The
Army of
Wolves

CLAIRE MOORE

BOOK ONE IN *THE HALF-GOD WAR* SERIES

Readers' Club Download Offer
Join my Readers' Club and get a free copy of my short story, "Atlanta"

www.clairemoore.co.uk/atlanta

Prologue

THE OLD WORLD ENDED, and nature took her revenge. Earthquakes and tornados, biting ice and fierce heat, bullets of hail and lightning that ripped open the sky. Glorying in their terrible celebration, the elements destroyed and cleansed and were only sated when all that mankind had made and unmade on Earth had gone.

Cradling the aching scars of their loss, the ragged remains of humanity took a long, painful breath. Drawing together into tribes, they looked back to the land and did what they did best—they survived. But just as they glimpsed the hope of a new future opening to them, an endless night swallowed the Sun.

With nothing else left and with their race on the cusp of extinction, they fell to their knees and prayed. From the depths of the darkness they prayed. To every God. To any God. The old Gods didn't listen. They were sick of man. Sick of lessons never learned, of history whirling over and back on itself like a leaf caught in the wind.

They were done.

Except for one. One ancient being who had been long forgotten and was long asleep. Hearing mankind's desperate pleas, the great God Chaos' nostalgia roused him from millions of years of stasis. The Earth looked nothing like he remembered. The swirls of green and blue were gone; the lands were scrunched together into a giant black island circled by a flat, grey sea. The human survivors were bedraggled; backward, a different species from those he once knew. Only one thing remained that he recognised—their mortality and their need; their constant need.

"Help us, Gods of the heavens, the future and past, help us to live. Help us. Help us…"

Chaos woke his daughter, Gaea and commanded her to help him restore the Earth to life, but Gaea told her father that she would only do as he willed if he agreed to a great sacrifice. He must let her send her own bloodline to live among mankind. These children of Gaea would give up their immortality to bring stability and regeneration to Earth. Chaos' son, Erebus heard these plans and insisted that his legacy should not be left out. He argued that Gaea had always been the favourite, that they needed the balance he could bring and that his dynasty would be important to this new world too…

So, with Chaos' nod, Gaea pushed away the darkness and the Sun blazed out of the night. The hulk of land blossomed with trees, grass and fields of flowers and the oceans glimmered, spinning with new shoals of fish.

Through the bloodlines of Gaea and Erebus, a new

generation of Gods became mortal. Remembering mankind's history of disrespect towards nature, these half-Gods strived for balance. They designed a great capital city, constructed with turquoise bricks that were like trees, rooted deep into the earth. These buildings were at one with their environment and lived in harmony with their inhabitants. Under half-God leadership, the humans protected the city and its surrounding forests and mountains. They farmed and fished just enough and looked after the land. Life became a perfect balance of give and take, and during this bright new era the citizens thrived.

For centuries, Chaos celebrated the equilibrium he created, and in his arrogance, he saw too late the threads of discontent and veins of avarice spreading like a rot through Erebus' bloodline. With mortality came mortal flaws, and these half-Gods followed the pull of selfishness and of greed. Wrangles and disputes split the two ruling houses of Gaea and Erebus. Bitterness and recrimination escalated into plots, assassinations and war... and after many years of bloody battle, the balance of power tipped towards the children of the shadows.

Chaos' disappointment swirled over the Earth like an ache, but Erebus' half-God children cut him off, thinking they didn't need him and that they knew better. Chaos turned away, for good this time, vowing never to look back as the descendants of the underworld crushed Gaea's bloodline, taking the crown for themselves and bringing darkness to the Earth once more.

Chapter One

The Pitch

"**I**F YOU DON'T WANT me to hurt you again you need to tell me where you got it," Eris said, dangling an empty glass vial from her long fingers. "Who's bringing in the drugs?"

"I…I don't know!"

The fury of Eris' fist jerked the girl's head backwards and forwards like a pecking bird.

Total darkness filled this tiny interrogation cell, as it did everywhere else in the Pitch. The girl had no idea when and how the kicks and thumps would reach her, but Strife could see the blows coming, each and every one. Not because of the night-vision lenses he had the privilege to be wearing, but because he knew all his mother's moves, the way she hit, the series of kicks that she preferred; their angle; their weight. The girl wriggled on her thin metal chair, her arms and legs clamped together with crisscrossing ropes.

Fresh screams flowed past him like scudding

clouds. Another broken rib. It had to be. Eris liked to snap them one by one, proud of the fact she never punctured a lung unless she wanted to.

He didn't believe this girl had any real link to the dealer; he knew that she was just another addict trying to get by. The signs were there—the scars on her eyelids, the burnt fingers, and the smell, like sweet, chargrilled flesh. A few more years of abuse and the light would burn away her retinas. The addicts didn't care, and why should they? If you were imprisoned for life in the Pitch, you'd never see daylight again anyway.

Nemesis shuffled next to him and he glanced up at her, seeing her discomfort in the set of her jaw.

"You must know something." Eris' voice was soothing now. "You acquired the drugs from someone, didn't you?"

"My cellmate, she got us two light vials, traded them, you know for her… her body." She looked away, shame sucking her chin to her chest. "We shared them, the flashes of light; the Sun in the vials, it's so beautiful. It's all we have to look forward to. One of the guards made the trade, but he hardly spoke and the darkness… the Pitch… how can I tell you what he looks like when I can't see?"

"Are you trying to make a fool of me?"

"No, Your Majesty!"

The back of the girl's head hit the floor with a crunch, her thin face exploding with colour as Eris crushed a foot down onto her throat.

Say something, name a name, anyone will do.

Closing his eyes, Strife hoped his thoughts would reach her, that she would stop being so honest and she would learn to play the game. A horrible gargle reminded him that he had no power of the mind, no powers at all in fact. He was a sixteen-year-old half-God boy bearing witness to a terrible crime and the girl couldn't speak even if she wanted to, because just a fraction more pressure from Eris' boot would snap her neck like a twig.

A thickness spread from his head down into his stomach, a feeling of panic that made him dizzy. As he rested his hand on the wall to steady himself, Nemesis stared at him, raising a thick, dark eyebrow.

It had been years since Eris had carried out this kind of menial interrogation, since she'd shown any flicker of interest in flash addicts or dealers, or even contraband that came into the Pitch. Strife had no clue why the queen was even here, why *any* of them were here.

The noises were becoming unbearable, a guttural wrenching for air, elbows and heels thumping against the floor. The charcoal identity drawing of the pretty freckled face that had smiled at him from the girl's prison parchment no longer registered as this bag of bones choking in the dirt.

"Mother," Strife whispered, "you're killing her."

"And?" Eris said.

"Maybe you should take a rest, my sister?" Nemesis said, stepping between them. "If you kill her now then all this effort... all *your* effort to get the best from this careful interrogation will just go to waste."

"Don't patronise me, Nemesis. What do you care about this flash addict's life?"

"I don't care anything about *her*, Your Majesty. I care about the information you require and that perhaps we should try a different approach to get what you need."

Eris' fists unclenched, and she eased back, smoothing down her long blonde hair with long pale fingers. The girl coughed, hacking into the dirt, sobbing and retching.

"Very well, Nemesis; you give it a try. I've had enough of the stink in here anyway. I'll give you half a turn to get her to talk."

A farewell kick to the girl's head unleashed an animal shriek that made the insides of Strife's stomach swill like stagnant water in the bottom of a bucket.

"What's with the grey face, Strife? You should be used to this by now," Eris said, looking him up and down. "I'm heading back to the castle. Nemesis, bring your report to me in the Pinnacle Room by noon."

"Of course," Nemesis said.

Eris bashed on the cell door and the guard scuttled in.

"Hail, Queen Eris!" he said, bowing and pressing his fist to his chest.

Ignoring him, she swirled out of the room and disappeared into the darkness.

"Right, let's get on with this, shall we? Could I have a set of night-vision lenses, please?" Nemesis said, holding out her hand and throwing the guard a sabre-toothed smile.

Thickset with an enormous square head, the guard stared from Nemesis to the mess on the floor of the cell, no doubt contemplating the fact that he would be the one left to clean it up later.

"Are yours faulty?" he said, his leg protectors squeaking against fat thighs as he lumbered on the spot.

"They are for our prisoner; just pass them to me and get out."

The guard hesitated.

"Have you forgotten who is in charge here?" Nemesis said.

"No, it's just most unusual for prisoners to have access to…"

"What's your name?"

"I… my name is Damon."

"Well, Damon, it's been a long, busy day. I'm tired, and the prince here is tired. We're fed up with the sight of bodily fluid and would like nothing better than a comfortable chair and a little bit of calming music to take our minds off the traumas of this hideous cell. Maybe *you* can help us get to that a little sooner? Now that I have your name, I'd be very happy to tell the queen that you are the right person for her to speak to about contraband and about human guards taking advantage of vulnerable young girls in this section of the prison. Is that what you'd like me to do?"

"No, madam," the guard said, thrusting something into Nemesis' outstretched hand. "Here, take the lenses!"

"Some water too please, if you will. Your canteen is fine."

Yanking the metal bottle from his belt, he held it out like a sacrificial offering.

"Wonderful; very kind of you," she said. "Now if you'll just give us some privacy, we'll let you know when we're ready to leave."

"Very well," the guard said, glancing at Strife again before clanking out of the cell.

Nemesis frowned at the closing door, her night-vision lenses tinting her beautiful hazel eyes with a splash of green.

"No wonder she has these problems when she insists on employing idiots. Now let's see what we can do with this poor specimen, shall we? Help me to untie her and get her up onto the bed."

The girl sobbed as they freed her from the chair, placing her as gently as they could onto the stained mattress. Wheezing, she clutched at the imprint of Eris' boot decorating her neck. They stood aside, heads bowed, letting her scrape back a particle of dignity as she snatched for shallow breaths. A mess of blood marked the place where her nose should be, and one of her hands was hooked into a broken claw.

"What's happening, Nemesis?" Strife said. "Why are we here? This girl... I looked at her file, Eris made me read it, and she was feverish with anger as she handed it to me. I pretended to see what she did, but I couldn't understand why this poor girl is being so harshly punished? This prison is filled with addicts.

None of them gets my mother's boot in their face."

"Your mother has convinced herself that this girl is somehow linked to a guerrilla cell, that she is part of a high-level plan to overthrow our dynasty."

"Is she?"

"No, Strife, she happened to have a negative thought after being force-fed those disgusting truth herbs, that's all."

"People have negative thoughts all the time, but they don't end up being interrogated by the queen and branded a traitor."

"They do when their uncle fought in the revolutionary wars."

"She's a half-God?"

Nemesis nodded.

He stared at the quivering mess on the bed.

"Phoebe… that's her name. It's the same as one of Asclepius' high commanders. Is that what Eris wanted me to see in the file?"

"Maybe," Nemesis said, shrugging.

"Does the girl know?"

"She thinks she's human, has no clue that she's a descendant of the great Goddess Gaea."

"But the truth herbs don't work on half-Gods, how did my mother get all that stuff for the files?"

"Eris doesn't need truths to do what she likes, she never has."

Nemesis scooped her long, brown dreadlocks up into her hand, tying them away from her face, making her cheekbones look even sharper. "And now she's just another mess that we're left to deal with."

"This guerrilla cell, is that just lies and paranoia too?"

"Now *that* is a different story."

She sat down next to the whimpering girl, her fur-lined leathers creaking. "Something is afoot; I can smell a shift, a rumble, but whoever, whatever is going on, they are managing to keep well under the radar, and it's driving Eris insane. She's going after anyone with a link to former rebels, getting them thrown into the Pitch for the smallest of misdemeanours. All her parchment analyses and torture have only made her more confused. It seems there are half-Gods hidden all over the city and beyond, most of them with no idea who they are. What you've just witnessed is Eris taking out all her frustrations on the thing that is nearest to hand. This poor girl is a punching bag, nothing more."

The revolutionary wars had ended with a series of mass executions that still gave Strife nightmares a decade later. He'd been forced to watch them all, a young boy, standing stoic at his mother's side, trying not to see, sending his mind somewhere else—anywhere else—as he stared at the beheadings, burnings, and hangings. There were so many that after a while they became one large blur of screams and blood.

"The rebels knew the end was coming back then, Strife. Their leader, Asclepius, he was smart. The younger ones, some went missing, many were never registered. He realised their ignorance would be the best way to protect them." Nemesis beckoned him closer, and he knelt beside her, watching as she stroked the girl's matted hair.

"They hid their children," Nemesis said, whispering deep into his ear, the smell of her breath a mix of lavender and raw meat. "Changed their identities, made them disappear. A few, like this girl, have been weeded out, but there are many more. Eris made a mistake. She was too pleased with herself, too jubilant in her victory, she didn't tie up every loose end, and now she's furious with herself for it."

"So, what happens now, with this girl?"

"We get this done. We do our job."

She dropped a pair of lenses into the girl's eyes.

"Have a look around; don't be afraid," Nemesis said, helping the girl to sit up. "Here, drink some water."

The girl sucked at the canteen too fast, choking most of it back up again.

"Go slow," Nemesis said.

Clutching the flask in her good hand, the girl nodded, taking smaller gulps.

"I haven't seen a face for so long I'd almost forgotten how one was put together," she said, blinking at Strife.

"Do you know who we are?"

"You are the queen's sister, and that is Prince Strife. No other half-God in Eristonia has such shiny black curls and eyes the colour of summer violets."

Tears fizzed behind his nose as the girl smiled at him with bloodstained teeth.

"We are here to help you. Your given name is Phoebe, is that correct?" Nemesis asked.

"Yes, that was my name before… before here."

"We only have half a turn to speak, Phoebe, and for you to tell us everything you can about the guard who gave you the light vials."

"I…I told the queen all I know. The dark here, it's so thick it clings to you; it gives you terrible claustrophobia, it confuses things…"

"This guard, did he touch you?"

"My friend, she sold for me too. He wanted me first, but she wouldn't let me do it."

"Did he grab you? Take hold of your clothes?"

Phoebe coughed, the pull of it wracking through her chest, flecks of blood peppering her chin.

"He did touch me; he rubbed himself against me," she said, shuddering. "I pushed him away, I…I shouldn't have let her do what she did. I was glad of the darkness then, when it started, glad that I couldn't see."

"Would you mind if I took away a little of your smock, Phoebe? I'm sure that if I can find his scent in your clothes, I'll be able to find him too, then I can give his name to the queen."

"You could do that?"

"You must know a little of my history, Phoebe?"

She nodded, "You have a… a strange bloodline."

"How delicately put! Yes, that's right; I have some animal genetics, wolf to be precise. Our pure-God ancestors did like their little perversions. But mutant genes can be very useful," Nemesis said, smiling. "My sense of smell is exemplary."

"I…" Phoebe coughed again as she tried to move her broken hand. "I can't reach."

"Don't worry, I can rip off a corner. Now, hold still."

Nemesis tore away a square of Phoebe's smock and held it to her nose. "Thank you, Phoebe, this will help. One other thing about the noises you heard. The guard, he must have made some sounds. Did you recognise the tone of them at all? Would they be from a deep voice or one with a lighter pitch?"

Phoebe wrinkled her nose as she tried to think, her expression girlish, reminding Strife how young she was.

"A deeper sound. Maybe a little gravelly, like someone older perhaps?"

"Great, that should give me what I need. I think I can take it from here."

"What… what will happen to me now?"

"You've done brilliantly. Have a rest for a moment and we'll get you to the hospital wing."

Stepping away, Strife closed his eyes as Nemesis settled the girl onto the stinking bed.

There was no hospital wing. Not in the Pitch.

"Thank you," the girl said in a whisper as Nemesis smiled down at her. "For letting me see, even for a while. It's strange, but having my eyes back did help me to remember…"

A flick of Nemesis' sharp nail against the skin of Phoebe's neck let loose a gush of liquid into the mattress. Phoebe's legs twitched and the water from her round, surprised eyes mingled with a stream of blood from her mouth.

"Shhhh," Nemesis whispered. "Don't fight it. Sweet dreams, Phoebe."

The fuzz of threatening tears escaped, and Strife let them have their silent run as he watched the girl bleed to death in the arms of her assassin. He knew this was the best way; better than being a cripple in the Pitch, better than dying a slow death from internal injuries in a filthy cell. Still, it barbed his heart to watch this girl's demise, the pointlessness of it all and the fact that he had now witnessed so many deaths that he'd started to forget their faces. That terrified him most of all.

Sliding away from the body on the bed, Nemesis wiped her blood-crusted hands on her leg protectors.

"It's done," she said. "Let's go."

"I…I don't know how much longer I can do this; be part of this," he said, his words bursting from him like a stagnant gust of air.

"Stay strong, Strife. We are all joined, all part of the same clan and the same set of equalisers." She took hold of his shoulders as he swallowed back fresh tears. "One day your mother's life circle will connect with those she has tortured and killed and righteous justice will come to her in this world or the next. Until then we must keep on living as best we can," she nodded towards the girl, "and provide a good death when we can."

He knew, for the most part, that she was right, but his heart wanted to scream that there had to be another way. They couldn't just sit around and wait for fate to play its hand, they had to have some control over their destiny and those around them or what was the point? What was the point of any of it?

Nemesis' expression remained blank, but her eyes glittered, reading him, taking in all she could see and smell and hear. Processing him in a way that made him shiver because it reminded him too much of his mother.

"The winds are shifting, Strife. Soon all this," she gestured to the dead girl still bleeding out on the bed, "will be gone."

"How do you know that? *What* do you know?"

Putting a finger to her lips and shaking her head, she nodded towards the door.

"I can smell one of the guards lingering outside. Let's get back to the castle. I will speak to your mother then start my search." She gave the slice of cloth another sniff. "I think I know which vile human this stench belongs to and I won't be quite so sad to see your mother's boot on his face."

"Are we just going to leave her like that?" he said.

"I'll straighten her out."

She unhooked the girl's bruised legs, crossing her arms over her chest. A prayer fell from his lips as Nemesis closed the girl's eyes with a brush of the same fingernails that had killed her.

"Go well into the next world, Phoebe. Go well and prosper."

"Amen," Nemesis said, spitting into the dust. "And let's hope for all our sakes that it's a whole lot better than this one."

Chapter Two
Training Grounds

A WHISTLEWHORP GREETED STRIFE at the entrance to the training grounds. Perched on top of the tall metal gates, it raised its yellow chest proud to the sky and warbled its disjointed song. Early morning sunshine glimmered from the bashed copper motifs of swords, hammers, and axes decorating the jagged fence which curled into thick trees. A feeling of weightlessness drifted up under his heels. The training grounds had become his own special kind of light-vial—his escape and his lifeline. Closing his eyes, he enjoyed the lilting music and the shiver of dew that prickled the air.

A small, rusty door opened at the bottom of the gates, startling the tiny bird, which darted away on invisible currents of air. "Good morning Prince Strife," the guard said, moving aside to let him pass. "An early start today?"

"Never too early to train."

"Aye, there is nothing better than a good fight to clear the passages and shine up the soul," the guard said.

"There's truth in that," he said, smiling when the guard bowed as he passed. The way the guards spoke and their old-fashioned formality were part of the reason why he loved it here.

Beyond the gates, the armoury welcomed him. A large, wooden building with a straw roof; its simplicity like a soothing balm compared to the cold prism glass of his mother's castle. He stood for a moment, as he always did, in front of his father's mounted sword. Kratos had disappeared so long ago he didn't even hold a place in Strife's memories. All he had were the stories. Tales of great military prowess and of the sword and chain that Kratos would take into every fight, the metal singing a song of slaughter as it whistled across the battlefields. The chain was long gone, but his curved sword with its hilt of sapphire remained here, framed in a glass box like a shrine. Whispering a silent prayer of courage to the father he never knew, he touched his fingers to his brow before turning away.

Running his hands along a row of shields, he drifted past shelves of weapons, watching the dust ruffle up in waves under his fingers. When he'd first come here, he had been slow and clumsy, a poor swordsman, winning fewer than one match in ten. The guards had scrutinised his early fights. With his dark skin and hair, he looked like his father, and they were hopeful he might show signs of his father's brilliance with a sword too. But their watchful eyes and their expectations made

.ervous, and he got worse, not better.

Until he met Zephyrus.

All humans had to complete a basic weapon-training programme, giving them just enough teaching to be useful to Eris as battle fodder. But Zephyrus' skills singled him out. His sword moved faster and with more accuracy than many of the guards and Strife had observed his craft with envy.

After weeks of trying and failing to copy Zephyrus' moves, he realised that he too was being watched. Zephyrus caught his arm as he'd tried to scuttle away, asking him if he wanted a partner, telling him that he needed more practice, that you couldn't learn anything on your own, and that he could help. And that's how it started; how their friendship began.

Even with Zephyrus' support, the training was hard. Physical fitness, that came easy, but his mind did not display the same agility. He couldn't let go, couldn't let the connection flow from brain to body to create that crucial dialogue that would get him a shot on target. Zephyrus told him to loosen his mind, but Zephyrus didn't understand. If he unclenched his mind, he would also wake the horror of his memories that he'd bolted away so well and for so long that he couldn't risk them bursting free; he couldn't risk the carnage they might bring.

With infinite patience, Zephyrus put together hundreds of exercises, spent hours with him in the yard, making him repeat sets of moves over and over until the spot of ground he stood on wore away to a dusty hole.

And the terrors locked in his head didn't spin free and fly screaming into the world as he had feared. While they worked, and as his fighting skills improved, the very opposite happened. A new light shone on the box of nightmares, fading them away, pushing him to work harder, to get even better so he could beat the wounds inside him as well as his opponents in the field.

Zephyrus made him someone different—someone braver and stronger, someone with great skills and a winner of victories. A person he could like, that he could even be proud of, that his *father* could have been proud of. And Zephyrus became more important to him than anyone, usurping Nemesis, who had always been his childhood protector. Because Zephyrus gave him all the things he never thought he'd have, he gave him trust in another his own age—a friendship of equals.

Selecting his favourite dagger from the metal racks, Strife sliced it through the air, enjoying the press of it against his palm. His sword glinted from the corner shelf, diamond steel with an emerald hilt, light and clean. Unlike the other weapons, swords were claimed and kept. Zephyrus had told him that a sword found its owner, that it knew where it belonged, that there was an unspoken commitment between blade and warrior. And as soon as he'd seen this one, *his* diamond sword, it had pledged itself to him and he to it.

With its weight in his hand, he felt graceful and calm, wishing that the person he became here was the real Strife rather than the frightened boy who lived like a ghost in his mother's castle.

Five different training grounds splayed out from behind the armoury each one housing a mix of terrains and a variety of beasts to battle. A large dirt-crusted wooden map gave you a hint of what to expect inside. The grounds were caged and meshed so they could mimic dozens of possible combat situations and hold all kinds of creatures. A bat marker flapped in the wind on training ground one, and a dead mole had been nailed to training ground five. He'd underestimated that one before. The moles were not animals but dozens of underground opponents using guerrilla tactics. He'd survived by hiding in a mud pool and watching each of their movements for hours to work out how to defeat them. One of the guards had given him his first nod of approval when he'd stumbled, exhausted but triumphant, out of the gates that day.

Two of the grounds were no longer in use; the guards posted here numbered fewer than fifty, and all the trainees were humans on the basic schedule. Full of mistrust after the revolutionary wars, Eris had created a new kind of militia, feeding select recruits a potion that would make them scream for days. Many died, but the strong ones—the unlucky ones who survived—were no longer half-God or human. These creatures, her Red Guards, had eyes the colour of the Sun, could turn their swords into fire and followed Eris' orders without question.

The human soldiers, the core of her army a decade before, those who had fought for her and watched their brothers and sisters die for her were forgotten. Their reward for their sacrifices? Those without a trade were cast out to work the mines in the frozen north beyond the mountains. Pleas to stay with families were met with death or a life sentence for disloyalty in the Pitch. Their memories of Kratos were what kept the remaining guards here. And so, after many months searching the training grounds for some way to bring him closer to his father, he realised that it had been right in front of him all the time, in the respect shining from the eyes of the men left behind.

Scanning the map, he spotted a rare symbol, a fire-red eye circled by wings. A dragon. They'd been breeding a few for fighting, and he'd never battled one before. His sword felt good, his arms strong, his spirits high. A perfect day for a new conquest.

Entering the central gate, which branched off into a pentagon of covered walkways, the guard on duty raised his eyebrows as he headed towards training ground three.

"Good choice, but not easy. Nocturne's already inside," the guard said. "He might appreciate some help."

"I'm already there," he said, picking up his pace.

The track opened to a miniature forest with fast-flowing rivers and waterfalls. Thwacking through the bushes, he hesitated, realising he had no idea which way to go.

"Nocturne! Where are you?"

"Rope!" A voice called from ahead of him. "Get the rope!"

A surge of rancid water piled down through the canopy, smashing him into a tree, grinding his ear against its trunk. His sword dangled uselessly from his hand as he wiped the wetness from his eyes, trying not to gag from the stink of fish and stagnant water. Distracted by a slink of metal, the water dragon snarled, lumbering away from him towards the noise, swinging its huge belly from side to side. Scanning the floor, he spotted a backpack decorated with a crescent moon and a coil of gold spilling from the top. Dropping to his knees, he grappled with the fastenings, yanking the rope free and stumbling towards the mossy banks of a fast-flowing river. Nocturne's quick blade snicker-snackered against the thing's scaly legs and water churned over the top of his chest as the dragon's spiked tail swung closer and closer.

"Throw it!" Nocturne said. "I can't hold him much longer!"

The waterlogged ground shifted and he snatched the rope closer to his chest. Whirlpools were spinning out across the river, swirling past jagged rocks. Another torrent of water erupted from the dragon's snaggletooth jaws, hitting Nocturne face-on, driving him under. The creature grinned, exposing rotten gums furred with algae.

Whipping the circle of gold over his head, he tried to keep steady, doing just as Zephyrus had once taught him with an old length of leather in the armoury, one smooth movement, round and round.

The rope sung, thwooping against the air.

Nocturne choked from the waves as the dragon

raised its leg. Its eyes twinkled, staring straight at him as its thigh wobbled above the foam. An expulsion of water and a crash of its foot would create a mini-tsunami large enough to drown them both.

Nocturne chased the silver swirl of his sword as it curled away from him, caught up in the current.

Flicking his wrist, Strife let the rope fly free, and the angle was flawless.

"I've got him!" he shouted, jumping and slithering in the mud. "Nocturne, it's over; I've got him."

Then the dragon smirked and ducked his head.

"Hell's gates!" he cursed, sliding to his knees across the sludge. "Get out of the river, Nocturne. Get out now!"

Then something sparkled, a flash of metal bursting through the dragon's thick green throat. Its head crunched back and the rope swooped in a perfect circle around its jaws. Jets of water squirted from its nostrils as it staggered, teetering onto one leg before smashing face-first into the waves.

"*Now* we've got him!" Nocturne said.

"Yes," he said, leaning against a tree to catch his breath, his heartbeat thumping in his ears. "We got him."

As he waded out of the river, Nocturne's long, black hair hung in a sodden mess down his back, and his smile caught at the claw of wrinkles that framed his weathered face. A grin exploded across Strife's cheeks, and the adrenaline ebbed from his body as they took hold of one another's shoulders and laughed.

"We make a good team," Nocturne said. "Zephyrus

taught you well."

His name sent a grey mist into Strife's mood, and his smile faltered.

"You know this is serious stuff, Strife. This level of fighting. You should help to train others; become a guard yourself."

"I don't know if I could."

Nocturne stood back into the dappled shade of the willow trees, watching him. "You should decide soon; your childhood is nearly behind you, and your mother will have expectations."

"I'm well aware of her expectations. You have no idea what I had to do in the Pitch yesterday. I don't want to talk about her. Don't spoil this, Nocturne." He turned away, sploshing into the river to wash dragon slime from his clothes. "I come here to escape all that; I come here for some peace."

"Sure, I understand," Nocturne said, bowing his head.

Strife sighed as the cold water spiked up around his knees and his heart filled with nails.

"I'm sorry," he said. "I guess I've no idea what I'm going to do. I'm not sure I have any say in the matter. My mother will decide, as always."

"There are other options," Nocturne said, nodding towards the forest. "Better ones."

Following Nocturne's gaze, he spotted a silhouette in the greenery, and his hand dropped to the hilt of his sword.

The shape turned into a scrub of blonde hair and a

dirty green tunic.

He grabbed Nocturne's sleeve. "Am I... Am I seeing things?"

"No; go, quick, there isn't much time."

As he raced through grasping branches his breath felt thick and claggy.

Standing with his back to a tree, Zephyrus raised his bronze sword and his head twitched, checking all around him, his nerves bright in his cheeks.

"Zephyrus!" he said, throwing his arms around his friend, hugging him hard. "You came back!"

"Strife, it is so good to see you," Zephyrus said, gently pushing him away and examining him. "You look older; stronger too!"

"I come here to the training grounds most days now, I... by the Gods, what does that matter? Zephyrus! You are here! Where have you been?"

"I...I don't have long. Nocturne thinks someone might be following me."

"Why would anyone be following you?"

"You have to take this." Pulling something from his pocket, he pressed it into Strife's palm. "And I have to go."

"You can't just leave again! Can't you stay? Can't we talk?"

Zephyrus shook his head. "We will, soon, I promise. I shouldn't have come here but I wanted to give this to you myself so you know that it's real. Soon we will have all the time in the world. You are ready; you are ready for this."

"Ready? Ready for what?"

Wind whistled through the trees, a gust of it catching at his spine.

"I have to go."

"No, please!"

Zephyrus turned away from him, running, and dissolving into air.

"Zephyrus!" The empty forest swallowed up his call and a bird chirruped once then fell quiet. Looking behind him, he searched for Nocturne, but he had gone too.

Swiping tears from his cheeks, his eyes throbbed in their sockets as he opened his fingers to a folded parcel of paper filled with wonky, black script. Written words had been banned from human use for over a century, yet here they were, scrawled on a white square of impossible sitting in his hand.

Strife swivelled from his bed to face the wall of windows overlooking the sleeping Flowlands sprawled far below him. Blinking at the sparkle of distant lights, his eyes were grainy with insomnia. Firing up the lantern beside him, the view disappeared, replaced by his own reflection. Hours of turning in his bed had twisted his unruly black curls into a bundle of knots. Screwing up his nose, he frowned, his dark skin looked grey and his large violet eyes were framed with red.

Gods, he looked so *small* perched on the side of his rumpled bed.

He snuffed out the light again with his fist.

Concealed by darkness, he kicked his bedclothes away, standing up to rest his hot face against the cool glass of the window. Castle Discord boasted the best views in the city and the beautiful turquoise buildings of the Flowlands were sprawled out below him like a wide crystalline sea.

The City Museum called to him from the west. Once a monument to symmetry, its entrance doors were now slumped into the road, lopsided, sad and abandoned, just like the rest of the city. Guilt billowed through his stomach. He'd been spending so much time in the training grounds he had neglected the museum and it would be suffering for it. It used to be their secret place, his and Zephyrus' hideout, but he hadn't been able to face going there alone.

Thoughts of his friend made him want to scuttle back to his bed. Instead, his gaze trailed over to a solitary patch of shining white-gold sitting in the ocean of blue. The Memory Library. He hated it almost as much as he loved the museum. A parasite that thrived on stolen goods, growing fatter and fatter on its diet of human memories extracted by force and by law. Scowling, he pressed his closed fists together so hard that his fingers ached. A draft of air kissed his neck and bristled his nerves as he turned away from the view to face his large, empty room. A pile of discarded clothing surrounded his bed and a set of dusty shelves housed an even dustier goblet. Despite the huge fireplace of burning stars, it still felt cold. This was not his space; it was his mother's, just like everywhere else in the castle. That was why he had never bothered to do anything with it, because filling it with junk would never make it his own.

One painting loomed down at him, a compulsory portrait of his mother hanging close to the door, her white face glaring like an evil moon. Crouching down to scoop up an old tunic, he aimed it at her head and it caught on the corner of the frame, the arms dangling to cover two cold blue eyes.

Stupid. Stupid. A picture couldn't see.

A slash of red paint smirked at him from the bottom of the canvas.

Rushing forward, he held his sheets out in front of him like a shield, covering the portrait in a layer of white. Taking in a slow breath, he held it for a long time before squeezing the air out through narrowed lips. He shuffled backwards until his knees hit the bed again, forcing him to sit down.

The uncertainties of the real world made lassoing dragons seem easy. In the training grounds, you fought and you won or you lost—simple. Alliances were clear, fights were fair, and there were no interrogation rooms, no truth herbs, and no torture. The sharp corners of the folded square of paper were still digging into his palm. This gift from Zephyrus blurred all that clarity and he didn't like it; he didn't like the change it might bring. Dragging his fist over his thigh, he pulled it along his ribs until it reached the middle of his chest.

Who would have believed that words on paper, the great enemy of the queen, would turn out to be little more than a flimsy scrap of nothing, so frail that his sweaty skin was already melting the markings away? Hunching his shoulders, he cupped his fist with his other hand like a child protecting a small pet, gazing at the dirt under his thumbnail and the dried blood where he had been picking at the skin. Unpeeling his fingers one at a time, he brought them so close to his face they brushed his nose as they opened. He stared at the mess of white crinkles and inky black scrawls that were blurring the rules of his reality.

7am, tomorrow, Memory Library. Don't be late. Zephyrus.

That's all Zephyrus could think to say, after leaving him alone now for all these months?

A javelin of anger shot through him; he should forget Zephyrus, forget all of it, he should go and find his sword and fight out his rage back in the training grounds… his heart twanged against his ribs and a splash of sadness sloshed his sudden fury away, leaving him empty. Because no matter where Zephyrus had been or what he'd been doing or how many notes he wrote, Strife missed him; missed him so much he ached with it to the very roots of his teeth.

Delving through his clothes, he hopped into crumpled black leg protectors and shoved his head through his cleanest bodysuit.

He paused as he reached for the handle of his door.

It had to go; the note. He couldn't keep it.

The fire twinkled at him.

The paper flew for a moment. Graceful, like a

white bird from a world long forgotten. Then, the first star of heat took it and it whooshed into a tiny burst of flame which left blobs of light jiving behind his eyes.

He knew the real reason his mother got rid of paper, scribes and books from human hands. Burnt them, killed for them, and rooted them out of every home. Paper alone held no power; paper alone was fragile and easy to destroy. But when you filled paper with words… *that's* when it gained strength, *that's* when it morphed into steel.

That's when it could bring down empires.

Chapter Three

Zephyrus' Secret

S TRIFE'S FEET WERE SINKING into the soft road of
the Flowlands, the marks of his tread following
behind him like the footprints of an invisible
friend. The turquoise buildings lining the streets
radiated that special kind of silence that only came in
the hours just before dawn. The Sun peeked above the
horizon, its rays like the golden wings of a distant bird,
its dazzle making his tired eyes sting. He gazed at it for
a moment before blinking away his fatigue and
continuing his trudge towards the Memory Library.

Thoughts of Zephyrus churned in his head. How
much did he really know about him? That he was an
orphan? That he was a great fighter? That he had been
the first human in Eristonia willing to accept him
without fear, the one person willing to be his closest
friend, and the one person he thought he could trust.

Until he'd left him without even a word;
disappeared, vanished.

He'd been so sure of the strength of their connection that he convinced himself there *had* to be a good reason for Zephyrus' absence. Then, as days turned into weeks, his certainty ebbed away into misery. How could Zephyrus have deserted him like this? What could be so important that he didn't even say goodbye? The boy with exemplary fighting skills and the warmest of smiles, who could cheer the gruffest of the guards, became a mystery to him, a person with secrets. He stopped and let his feet clot with the road, thinking again about Phoebe, about Nemesis' words of hidden children, of change coming, and of Eris' fury because she sensed something too...

The crystal bricks of Castle Discord shot the Sun's first rays across the city like laser rainbows, blinding him for a moment until he found some shade. The building loomed over the Flowlands as a physical reminder of his mother's omnipotence. Could Eris be watching him now? Panic tickled at his throat as he glanced around for her winged spies—the oversized grey crows with their black eyes and razor claws that patrolled the skies, but it all looked clear.

If he turned back now it would be as though nothing had happened; he could go on with his life, head to the training grounds, and forget all of this with the swing of his sword.

But Zephyrus owed him an explanation; a big one.

And Nocturne. Nocturne was part of this too. Whatever *this* was. Besides, the note held no danger now he'd transformed it to ash in his fireplace.

Wiping away a streak of sweat from his forehead, he picked up his pace, hurrying now towards the Memory Library. As he jogged he saw something ripple like a mini heat haze in front of the library's tall white-gold doors. The street wrinkled as he skidded to a halt. Red Guards. Marching back and forth, three of them, watching the entrance. The tallest glided over like a sail in a brisk wind, passing its fire-sword so close to his face, he felt his skin tighten. It slammed the splayed fingers of its left hand hard across its chest, sending orange sparks flying.

"Hail, in the name of Queen Eris!"

"Hail!" His own hand returned the customary gesture, his palm thudding against his heart, the movement as automatic as breathing.

"Are you here to assist us, Prince Strife?" its voice fizzed and its crackling breath reeked of smelting ovens.

He shook his head, confused.

"With the truth potions, Prince Strife. It's Purification Day."

Purification Day? Gods, that's why the guards were here. They were patrolling the library, waiting for the hordes of humans to come herding through its doors. Purification Day. The day of the interrogation of their deepest thoughts, the day the Memory Library got fed. Dragging in a jittery breath, his tongue floundered as the guard stood waiting for his reply.

7am, tomorrow, Memory Library.

The message from the note was branded in his head. Did Zephyrus know what day he had chosen?

"I've come to observe," he said. "Please follow your usual procedure; just pretend I'm not here."

A smile bled from his face as the guard lingered.

Had it understood him?

"Dismissed?" he ventured.

"Of course, Your Majesty." The guard's eyes sparkled and his face exploded with heat. Nobody but his mother got called Majesty and this thing knew it. It bowed and slid away.

Scowling at his feet, he moved closer to the Memory Library doors, keeping his head down. If this were the training grounds he would finish off the guard with an ice-knife from the armoury stores. But this wasn't a drill, this was life in Eristonia, a horrible reality of his mother's making, a reality he usually did his best to avoid.

Vibrations buzzed up his legs as the Memory Library's shining gates yawned open. Groups of crows hovered inside like fat flies, their beaks clacking. Metal fencing laced the gold-tiled entrance hall, winding towards a large square room filled with rows of industrial-looking chairs that had clamps jutting from their arms. The truth potion caused some humans to have fits and the straps were there to hold them still, to keep their bodies fixed in place while their minds were clawed open like poisoned oysters. Scribes sat next to each chair, poised with their parchments, ready to record everything they heard.

People were appearing from houses and roads, their heads hanging as they trudged towards him. He tried to wait outside but the guards hissed at him, shuffling him through the doors. Running his fingers through his messy hair, he glanced with dismay down at his wrinkled leg protectors. One of the rancid crows circled him and his mother's voice wheeled inside his head like a harpy picking at a carcass.

"What are you doing presenting yourself to our subjects dressed in crumpled rags? Sixteen years old—almost a fully-grown half-God and you're a disgrace to our family name. A disappointment to the realm."

One more minute.

Zephyrus had one more minute.

Nibbling his bottom lip, he watched the mass of bodies enter the room, the guards rounding them up, steering them through the metal barriers. So many people. He *never* came to Purification Days, and why would he? Watching brains being scoured out like dirty cooking pots? No thanks.

Eristonia's citizens spoke in hushed tones as they weaved through the fencing that curled, snakelike towards the chairs.

"Is that the prince?" A man pointed, nudging the woman next to him.

"What's he doing here?" she replied.

"Looks like he's just got out of bed!"

The whole room turned to stare, the force of their gaze making his ears ring.

Sorry, Zephyrus, time's up. I'm leaving.

He shoved his way back through the bodies, desperate now to get out; he needed to be in the open, he needed to get some air, he needed to breathe.

"Wait!" A clear voice rang out above the whispers. "Strife! Wait!"

Turning to the room, the same sick feeling wavered in his gut, but this time fuelled by something else.

A hand shot above the throng, followed by a blonde head, jumping.

The crowd dissolved into a blur.

Zephyrus was right there, swimming through the mob towards him.

"Get back. No talking!"

Zephyrus hissed in pain as a guard sliced at him with their sword.

"Get in line!"

Wriggling forward, he slammed his hand against the tall section of fencing near Zephyrus' place in the line.

"Please, just wait for me," Zephyrus said, bashing the grills and touching their palms together for a moment. "I won't be long."

Nodding, his stomach merged with his feet as he trailed back from the fence, watching Zephyrus shuffle forward.

A shriek flew out from the front of the room.

A woman twitched and writhed in one of the chairs, its clamps were grinding deep into her head and her arms were in spasm, thrown wide and jolting like a tree in a lightning storm. She screamed again and a bell sounded, a guard zooming to her side. The room's sudden silence was sharp with anticipation.

"Full cleanse," the guard shouted, dragging the

woman from the chair by her shaking arms.

"No!" she said, sobbing and clutching at the purple bruised patches on her head.

Full cleanse. That meant the potions had found something; something inside this poor woman's mind that the queen would not like.

Zephyrus seemed to be gliding in slow motion towards the corner. His heart tripped against his stoppered throat and he pounded on the metal barrier.

"Zephyrus! Stop!"

Zephyrus ignored him, sliding into one of the chairs, the clamps seeking out his head like hungry worms. A guard tipped the truth potion into Zephyrus' open mouth. Their meeting in the training grounds would be there in his mind, there for the herbs to extract; an unforgivable act of treason which would incite the full wrath of the queen.

"Zephyrus!"

As he smashed his fists against the fence, the crowds parted and he staggered, dizzy, realising they had pulled back not to help him reach his friend but to create a direct path to the screaming woman about to be cleansed.

"Prince Strife, help me," she pleaded, pushing against the guard, one arm forward, her eyes glistening.

"Be quiet," the guard said. "Your thoughts have violated Code Five of the Conduct Directory. Your brain must be cleansed!"

"Please," she begged, children clustered around her knees like barnacles. "If they cleanse me they take everything. All my memories; everything. I won't remember my own children! It was just a dream," she sobbed. "I can't control my dreams."

All the heads in the room shifted towards him; expectant; hushed.

"Please, Prince Strife; please grant me pardon."

As the woman quivered in front of him his nerves curdled into anger. Why had Zephyrus dragged him here? Eris' rules were sacrosanct and a Code Five meant a serious breach; a memory involving plans linked to violence towards the queen triggered a full brain cleanse, with no exceptions.

"I need more information," he said. "Perhaps we can have another look at the memories, maybe they weren't transcribed correctly…"

"Cleansing must take place immediately," the guards said, hissing at him in unison. "With all due respect, Prince Strife, you do not have the authority to override a Code Five."

His body hollowed and he could feel the hope in the room slumping like a pair of weary shoulders. He blanked out the sounds of the woman's sobs as they dragged her away.

Zephyrus' sudden grip on his arm made him jump.

"Come on, Strife, I've finished. Let's go."

They weaved away from the grumbling crowds, ducking through the entrance doors and out to the main street. With Zephyrus by his side, the paths looked wider and the blue Flowlands seemed to sparkle.

"That… that poor woman," he said, glancing back.

"Shhh, Strife; it isn't your fault."

"You should be right behind her, getting your own memories decimated. How did you do it? How did you hide your thoughts from the potion?"

"We'll talk, but not out here. Let's go to the museum, it'll be safer there."

They ran, leaving the Memory Library far behind and he strained to match Zephyrus' speed, his legs pounding, but Zephyrus' feet were so quick that his imprints barely registered on the road.

"You've been eating too many royal banquets," Zephyrus said, jogging on the spot, waiting for him to catch up.

"That's unfair. You've got faster, that's all," he said, trying to regulate his breathing, not wanting to give away how much his lungs were burning.

They slowed when they reached the long column-lined boulevard leading to the museum. As they walked closer, his stomach dipped when he saw how much it had changed. Its bricks were rotting, spreading into the road, forming hardened puddles of blue syrup. It needed visitors, people bustling through its rooms, feeding it, watering it, tending to the roots that formed the foundations of its walls. Most of its windows had melted together so its façade now resembled a frowning face with scars for eyes.

Ducking under an arch of blue glass to the left of the main doors, they trotted down a tangled set of steps. Putting his hands to the walls, they warmed to his touch, delighted to see him, despite all his time away.

They pushed open a narrow door at the bottom of the stairs and squeezed through the gap. The old storage room still had a couple of training swords lying on the floor next to a large frayed rug. Picking one of them up, he twirled it in his hands. Zephyrus snatched up the other one and grinned.

"Shall we?" Zephyrus said.

Dust danced around them as they sidestepped and jabbed. A rivulet of sweat snaked down his back as he took the force of Zephyrus' sword, working extra hard to keep up with his friend who seemed faster and more sure-footed. It felt good to be back at the museum, just the two of them practising their moves, away from his mother, away from torture and pain and the stink of the Pitch…

His loneliness returned in a wave so strong he lost his footing and Zephyrus' blade touched against his heart.

"A good fight," Zephyrus said, his face serious.

They bowed and shook hands.

"Oh, I let you win," he said grinning and bashing Zephyrus' shoulder with his own. "Could have had you five moves ago."

Zephyrus laughed, nudging him back.

"Remember when the guards found that cyclops family hiding out on the edge of the city and chucked them all into the training grounds?" Zephyrus said, giving his sword a final twirl before resting it against the wall.

"They were really fast, surprisingly nimble on their

feet," Strife said. "And my, they were *stinky*!"

"Oh Gods, I remember! They were like thousand-year-old cheeses."

"You almost passed out; I had to dig out the smelling salts."

"You did not!"

"I did! You were swooning like a baby with a fever."

I won't remember my own children.

The face of the woman from the Memory Library filled his head, her thoughts about to be purged, her children clinging to her legs.

"Slander." Zephyrus' voice sounded like a distant hum.

Help me, Prince Strife; please grant me pardon.

His whole body burned with shame.

He'd done nothing to help that poor woman; nothing.

"Strife?" Zephyrus said, moving a step closer to him. "Are you okay?"

If Zephyrus had stayed away, he wouldn't have been anywhere near the Memory Library. He wouldn't have yet another piece of darkness to grapple with on his long nights alone. He'd only just got used to being by himself again; only just got past the terrible sickness of missing someone so much that the motions of daily living felt like a punishment from the old Gods. Zephyrus shouldn't have come back here with his messages and his new sword skills; he should not have come back acting as though nothing had happened.

"Strife? Are you unwell?" Zephyrus said, reaching

for him. "Why don't I help you to sit down?"

Snatching his arm away, he balled his hands into fists, his rage rising in his throat, sharp and fresh.

"Hell's Gates, Zephyrus, why are you here? Why did you make me go to the Memory Library? You know how much I hate it! And where have you been?"

"I had to go because I needed to put some things in place," Zephyrus said calmly. "These things were important to make sure that I could come back again but I had to keep what I was doing secret, I couldn't risk you knowing anything, I couldn't risk you accidentally giving it away. But I'm here now. I'm here for you, and I want you to come with me."

"You want me to leave the city? With you?" he asked, surprise sweeping away his anger.

"Yes."

"I don't understand!"

"All this time away from you, I've been training, with others... like me, like you."

He shook his head. "Others? What others? And like us how?"

"The truth potion, the memory-stealing that your mother inflicts on the humans, it doesn't work on half-Gods, does it? She's never really cracked that one... not yet."

They stared at each other in silence and his pulse thumped in his forehead.

"You're a half-God?"

"I know you wanted to help that woman, Strife. I saw it in your eyes."

Her screams; the pleading…

"Strife, are you listening to me?"

His only friend had been lying to him.

Familiar fingers of fear were creeping up on him like a slow tide.

"You must know the old traditions," Zephyrus said. "You know what a secret note means. The revolutionaries used it for generations. It's the way we ask, the sign, the way we ask someone…"

"To join with the rebel army," he said, his voice flat and cold. "To join the revolution as a spy."

Zephyrus nodded.

"So, is that what *you* are? A spy, sent here to dig out my secrets? A half-God version of the truth herbs?"

A flicker of shame shot across Zephyrus' face as he shook his head.

"No, it's not like that. I am one of many hidden half-Gods; one of the remaining generation of Gaea's bloodline. Only a few of us know who we are, but we do know about many others and we're starting to find them. We've found a safe place; a snowy realm, way beyond the northern mountains; a no man's land, outside of Eris' rule. There is a portal, Strife. A way to get there from Eristonia that your mother knows nothing about. We are gathering strength and numbers, preparing ourselves for war."

Secret places? Portals? War?

A rush of lightheadedness made him reach for the wall.

They hid their children. That's what Nemesis had

said, too. The rebels, the bloodline of Gaea; *they hid their children.*

"We can take back this city and this planet," Zephyrus said. "Return it to goodness, bring it back to Gaea; to democracy; to harmony!"

Zephyrus must be deluded. Did he believe a few hidden half-Gods could defeat his mother? Could bring back a world where Eris no longer ruled? A world with personal freedom, free speech and justice? Jealousy itched like a disease through his body. He had no truth and no belief, just his solitude and his sword.

"I don't know who you are anymore."

"I'm the same person. I'm your friend."

As he broke free from Zephyrus' gaze, his old sadness hit him like a bundle of needles spiking through his blood. He stared at the floor, trying not to be sick, trying not to cry, and trying not to think about never seeing Zephyrus again.

"You spied on me, lied to me, deserted me… how can you be my friend?"

"I know you, Strife. I really *know* you. You believe what your mother does is wrong; you hate the truth potions, the torture, and the fact all those innocents have been thrown into the Pitch. You can't hide away in the training grounds for the rest of time. You can't stand aside while your mother continues to terrorise and kill. So, I've come back here to seek your forgiveness and to get you away from this prison you call home."

"You knew the memory-cleanse was today, didn't you?" he said. "You arranged it on purpose to remind me just how insignificant I am."

"No, Strife. I wanted to show you why you need to stand up against your mother, to prove to you that you've got so much more courage than you think."

For a second, he saw it; he saw himself standing next to Zephyrus, like a real warrior, leading a gang of revolutionaries against his mother and her cruel regime. Saw the glimmering lights of the Flowlands restored to their former glory, the dying buildings growing tall again, the museum square and solid, the castle filled with brightness and with love…

"How can I join with you when you are of Gaea's bloodline? Gods, Zephyrus I am part of Erebus' dynasty. Our families have always been mortal enemies, we've been fighting against each other for generations and my mother… she… she's been looking for hidden half-Gods; she knows something isn't right. She'll *find* you!"

Zephyrus grabbed him. "We have to do this. *You* must do this, we can break the pattern, bring our two families together to end this misery and pain."

Could he? Could he stand up against his mother?

"But how will you fight her? She's got a thousand guards and the crows watching our every move. Her two generals, Alecto and Tisiphone have their own armies in every corner of the kingdom. Most humans and half-Gods are too terrified of a lifetime in the Pitch to even look her in the eyes. She's watching. She sees everything!"

Zephyrus smiled. "Not everywhere and not

everything, Strife! The portals, there are three in total—
one in the northern reaches, one in the mountains, and
the third hidden in the forests on the edge of Eristonia
near to the University of the Eight Spires. We've called
it the White Plains; our community in the north, our
world of ice and snow that is clean and fresh and new.
We can use the portal from the White Plains to get into
the city; to attack with our stealth and our brains. She'll
underestimate what we can do, just like we did with
those stinking cyclopes in the training grounds. And she
doesn't know about us, Strife, not yet. We have more
joining us every day; not just hidden half-Gods but
many of the human guards that she discarded after the
wars, the ones she sent to the mines, the ones she forgot,
they want change too."

"Nocturne?"

"One of the first."

His heart grew fat as he let himself catch hold of
Zephyrus' fire, allowing it to burn brightly inside him.
An army… a new world… Gods, what if there *could* be
a different future?

"You're considering it, aren't you? Oh, Strife, it's
the perfect time to help us. Nocturne knows you are
ready for this too. Though I still need to convince my
sister, she thinks—"

"Your *sister?*" Ice poured through his veins.

"Yes, that's where I've been. With my family, with
Alcyone."

"Your *family?* You told me you had no family. That
your parents died when you were six!"

"They did. They died a decade ago, in the same square we just left, right in front of the Memory Library. You saw them, your mother made their execution the grand finale of their failed war."

A memory flashed into his head, of his mother, her pale face impassive as the remains of her army marched up to the castle. They were bedraggled, bloody, and victorious.

"They'll pay for this, Strife," she'd said, grinning at him, her teeth clenched, her eyes narrowed. *"And you'll be my witness, alongside every other person in this city who ever dared to question my rule, in thought or in deed."*

She'd made him watch; made him watch them burn, the beautiful couple who had tried to change the world. They'd been holding hands. That's what he remembered in his nightmares, the way their grip never loosened, even as the flames ate away their flesh. His mother had rested her cool fingers on his shoulders so he couldn't turn his head away and he'd known he'd get a beating if he cried, so he'd stood stoic and sick to his stomach as they burned to ash. They were beautiful, Asclepius and Amphitrite, the rebel king and queen. After that execution, the truth herbs and the memory-cleansing started, then came the Red Guards and mass imprisonment for the smallest of misdemeanours. In those early years, just after the war, the Pitch had the highest population in the city.

"Your mother didn't know about my sister or me; we were never registered," Zephyrus said. "We stayed away from the city for many years, in the outer reaches of Alecto's territory, under the mountains, in places that hold no interest to royalty."

They hid their children.

Nemesis' words whirled around his head again, merging with his memory of Phoebe, that poor, broken girl, dead in a cell, her lifeblood soaking into a dirty mattress.

"They just made things worse, your parents," he said. "That's what war does, it makes things worse."

"That's because they lost. That won't happen again."

"You used me. You were spying on me."

"It started off like that," Zephyrus said. "But things change. We were... we *are* best friends."

"A sister," he said, shaking his head. "You made me believe that you were alone too, that you knew how I felt."

"I lost both my parents. I did understand; I do."

"Do you?"

Zephyrus' eyes crinkled with pain and he itched to give his friend a hug, to tell him it didn't matter, that he would help him, that he would go anywhere, do anything to be by his side, but a deep, dark, horrible part of him wanted Zephyrus to suffer for his lies.

"What about Nemesis? She's done all she can to protect me. I can't just leave her."

"You'll have to let her go. She is part of your mother's world and she'll always be entangled in that web. You must start fresh and make a new beginning."

"Nemesis has been my protector for years, she's

always been there, she's never left me. My father disappeared, then you... I won't do that to her."

"I understand," Zephyrus said. "You must go back to the castle then, go back one last time, go and see Nemesis, visit your mother, remind yourself of how things are, how things will stay if you don't come with me. You will say your goodbyes, then you will meet me back here at the twelfth turn of the hand, at the hour of pure night with your decision."

"*Tonight?*"

"Yes, tonight. If you don't know your answer by then you never will. Tonight at twelve. After that, I will be gone."

Zephyrus smiled, and he could see in that moment how much his friend cared for him and that he believed in this dream, this joining of their families. Hope filled Zephyrus; hope that he could be part of, that he could shine with too.

"Okay. Tonight, I'll see you at the twelfth turn."

"Or you could come now, Strife. Why don't you just come with me now?" Zephyrus' blue eyes blazed with a feverish light.

Could he leave now, run and never look back?

Then he remembered how he'd felt when Zephyrus had vanished—bitter and betrayed.

He owed Nemesis. He owed her a goodbye.

And his mother, what about his mother? He realised then that he needed to see Eris one last time, to send her a silent farewell, to have his own strange kind of closure before he turned his back on his family line, before he made her his enemy.

"I will be back at the twelfth turn of the hand. I promise."

"Then I will see you tonight," Zephyrus said, his eyes gleaming. "My brother."

Brother.

Strife hugged him then, hugged him tight and close before he turned and walked away.

Chapter Four
Alcyone

ALCYONE TRUDGED IN CIRCLES, re-tracking her footprints that were stamped deep into the thick snow of the far northern reaches of Eristonia. She stuck close to the portal, which she had marked with a triangle of black stones and a red-painted stake pounded into the snow. Banging her hands together, she tried to generate some heat. She could find this spot in her sleep but she still cleared the pile of rocks every morning to calm her morbid fear of losing sight of Zephyrus' road home. More flakes were falling like clumpy, fat stars, clinging to her pale eyelashes and her strawberry blonde curls as she scanned the bright white blast of land.

"Where are you, Zephyrus?" she whispered, her breath a hazy cloud. In their remote northern bolthole, the land and sky were difficult to separate. Shielding her eyes with her hands, she blinked into the brightness, its glare making her so dizzy that she had to stare at her feet for a moment to keep her balance.

"Alcyone!"

A dark shape wavered in front of the stones, a shape that fixed itself into her brother's grinning face. Taking hold of his hands, she enjoyed the familiar feel of them, of the halo of calluses across the palm of his sword hand and their warmth, their enduring warmth.

"Are you safe? Did anyone see you?"

"I'm fine," he said, giving her a hug. "You worry too much."

"So, is Strife joining us?"

"Yes, he is," Zephyrus said. "He just needs a few hours to go back to the castle to see Nemesis…"

"The deal was always that he came straight away, as soon as you told him."

"He's scared, Alcyone. I unloaded a lot of information on him. He needs to digest it a little, to say his goodbyes. And I respect that; it means that he's serious about it."

"What if he confesses everything, what if he gives us up?"

"He won't."

"You've let him saunter back into the castle after telling him all our secrets?"

"Have some faith."

"Some faith? Where did that ever get any of us?"

Taking hold of her shoulders, he leaned down, forcing her to meet his eyes.

"There are so few of us, Alcyone. We need a bigger army with trained recruits. The guards in the training grounds, they watch him fight, they know how good he is and they respect that; they can see his father in him. The old ones are restless, Red Guards have replaced them and they worry that they'll either be transformed into one of those monsters, or sent off to the mines. Worse, they don't feel trusted. Strife will bring them to us and he will help us make history by joining our families together. This will be the greatest symbol of hope any of our citizens will have had in many lifetimes."

Scowling, she pulled away from him. Strife the miracle worker; Strife the saviour of them all. What about Strife the executioner? Strife the son of the worst despot their world had ever known?

"Have your memories been altered, Zephyrus? He watched our parents die. He didn't even blink as they burned in front of him, his mother smiling by his side." She took a step backwards, the old hurt and anger bundling to the surface, forcing her to brush away tears. "We always hated him—both of us!"

"I did hate him… but then I got to know him, and he doesn't want the world to be this way. He is thoughtful, kind… good. The way he was at our parents' burning, it's a coping mechanism. Believe me, Alcyone, he's seen much worse than what happened to our mother and father. If he didn't blank it out it would turn him mad. He's a survivor, like we are."

"We must think about what's best for our *own* bright new soldiers who need stability and leadership here and now."

"I *am* thinking of them," Zephyrus said with a sigh, "and I would never put you in danger; you are my only family."

"I hope you're right," she said. "For all our sakes."

Grinning at her, he pulled a silly face and gave her shoulder a gentle shove. A smile itched at the corners of her mouth. He could charm anyone, her big brother, and he knew it. It seemed like a lifetime ago that she'd watched the same boy fight back tears as he headed off to a distant city to make friends with a reclusive prince.

"I am meeting Strife tonight at the twelfth turn of the hand," he said. "It will be my last chance to go to the city for a while. Nocturne has found me some weapons, including more of those lightweight throwing knives. I want to bring them back for you."

"I don't care about the knives and I don't want you to go away again. Can't you stay a little longer? I need you here with me!"

"You have enough strength for both of us, my sister. You are a warrior; a queen in the making, just like our mother."

"I don't want to have the strength for both of us. We work best together, as a team of two, as we always have. I hardly even remember our parents; you are the only thing that matters to me."

"I know that, Alcyone, but we have others to think of too, now."

"So, you're risking your life for Strife."

"I'm risking my life for the future, for all of us."

Shaking her head, she stared out into the distance,

letting the white take over, letting it sink into her head.

"Do you remember why we love this place? This wasteland of ice and snow?" Zephyrus said.

"Of course, I do, it's our sanctuary."

During and after the war, they had spent many years living underground, hidden in secret tunnels beneath the northern mountains. In the early days, there had been others there too—a small tribe of children, pretending to be older than they were, pretending not to miss their old lives, squashing in tears for absent parents who were fighting to make the world better for them. They made sleeping nests in the walls, surviving off what they could hunt or forage, comforting each other at the news of each new death. A mini community with the eldest member just shy of her eleventh year. After the war ended and their own parents' execution, the other children disappeared one by one, whisked off into adopted families, hidden in plain sight. Alcyone and Zephyrus refused to leave, refused to be separated from each other, refused to bury their memories of their mother and father. The archer Atlanta was sworn to protect them, and she kept them safe for many years, but one day the giant mountain bats took her too, and they stayed in their stony underground village alone.

The map of the portals had appeared from nowhere one night, tucked underneath her scratchy blanket. It had been made from the skin of some unknown animal and she found its leathery smell soothing, hugging it to her chest for many nights like a comforter. It sang to her too, a musical chime like metal flying through the wind. She didn't tell Zephyrus about it straight away. His restlessness had been growing around him like a noise and she knew that as soon as she showed him the map he would want to follow it. She, on the other hand, needed to take a little time, needed to hold on to it for a while so she could gather herself before they left their safe place and ventured back into the world. She wondered if it could be magic, left to her by faeries or a guardian angel watching over her in her sleep. The map revealed many new places that she never even knew existed, swathes of land far beyond the city and the mountains. There were three yellow stars marked on the map. One was not too far from them, the second in the middle of Eristonia, and the third sitting in the extreme north, way beyond the furthest of the iron mines.

As soon as she told him about the map, Zephyrus fixated on the stars marked on it, desperate to find the nearest one. They trekked for five days, across the spiky mountains, hiding in fear from Alecto's killer bats that hunted for prey every evening, swooping across the sky in a flurry of black. After so many nights away she was tired and scared and wanted to go back, but Zephyrus refused, fixing his face into an expression of stone-like determination. He believed the map had been sent to them for a reason, that the sound of metal chimes inside it matched the old stories of lost king Kratos and his musical fighting chains, and that if they had been given it by a *king*, then it had to be for a purpose, and they must keep going...

When they finally found the location of the star, they flagged. They were stuck halfway up a flat-topped mountain with sharp-leafed plants and a thin stream running through scraggy grasslands. The symbol on the map had no equivalent in the real world. They scrutinised the bark of the trees, dredged through the river, dug holes, scraped aside bushes... but found nothing. They argued then and she cried. What were they doing here? The map had taken them nowhere! Zephyrus turned his back on her, clenching his fists, making a sadness shimmer behind her eyes. Her tears were falling faster and faster and through the film of water, it appeared to her—a glow of light, a star of gold in the wavering air. With her wonder, her misery faded and the star faded too, so she pulled back the worst of her sadness through misty memories of her mother and father and the star shone brightly again. And she knew then what it needed. Grabbing Zephyrus' hand, she pulled him towards it, pain contorting her as it swallowed them up, sending them here. Sending them to the White Plains.

The desolation of their new land of ice and snow played tricks on Zephyrus' mind. He would see invisible shapes, ghosts and spirits that woke him screaming in the night, and she worried then that this had been some kind of horrible trick; that Kratos' spirit had sent them here to die.

She found them food and killed the beasts that prowled here for furs, and she taught Zephyrus how to fight the nightmares; showed him how to enter the cleanest, clearest section of his mind, to keep hold of it and to never let go. And as they worked together something happened—they built a strength of purpose that conquered every fear. And with this they began the next stage of their journey. They started seeking out their old friends from the caves, tracking down all the young people whose parents had died in the war and who had been adopted and hidden, finding them and bringing them back to the White Plains.

She kept the map close to her for many years, and sometimes, it still played its song of chains and chimes. But it never revealed its true origins to them, and as they planned their rebellion they decided it was too risky to keep it, so they destroyed it, burning it in their evening fire, raising a cup to it, their saviour, as it melted into kindling.

"The White Plains nearly broke me," Zephyrus said. "But you kept me going, you transformed us both, and you made this place our future. Strife's mind is full of ghosts too, and I must help him in the same way you helped me. Support him as he battles past his fears and overcomes the terror Eris has drilled into him. That's why I need you to understand, why I need you to be patient and wait just a little bit longer."

"Do I have any choice?"

"Remember how many nights you hung on to that portal map, how long it took you to be ready for the biggest journey of your life? That is exactly where Strife is now; he is clutching onto the tattered remains of his present and he only has a few hours to let it go. You of all people should understand that more than anyone."

Tears welled in her eyes and she hugged him tightly, her grown up, sensible brother, breathing in his clean smell of lemons and mint. She rested her head next to his; her only family and her life.

"Come back to me soon."

"I'll see you tonight and I'll have Strife with me."

She nodded, reluctant to pull away.

Squeezing her hand one last time, he stepped back into the triangle of stones and she watched his physical shape blur and flicker while he grinned at her, his blue eyes shining as he ported back to Eristonia. And she changed her focus to keeping busy, to getting through until he returned. She needed to work on her training plan for her new recruits and she needed something warm and comforting—a hot drink in her cabin…

Then as Zephyrus' face faded into swirls of fuzzy light, his smile slid away too, morphing into a contortion of pain.

"Zephyrus!" she called, reaching for him.

"Keep away! Don't follow me, Alcyone, *don't* follow me! I love you. I love you…"

"*Zephyrus!*"

His distant scream bit into her heart and she screamed too, grappling for him and sobbing as her arms closed around empty air.

Chapter Five
The Great Hall

S TRIFE CLIMBED THROUGH THE empty floors of Castle Discord, his brain a scribble of thoughts, jumping from Zephyrus to all the other children who were following the same road as their long-dead parents. Hundreds of them hidden away in the snow, training to fight for freedom, for democracy, for everything half-Gods and humans had been denied for so long. He still couldn't quite believe that Zephyrus wanted him to be part of it all too, and the dark portion of his mind reminded him that Zephyrus had lied to him, lied about his background and his parents. About Asclepius, the healer turned warrior, and beautiful Amphitrite, who commanded the seas. They were infamous; legends frozen in a history that his mother had tried so hard to scratch out. And a sister, Alcyone, both hiding from the registry somehow, just like Nemesis had told him, just like poor dead Phoebe. Their fathers had been mortal enemies, their opposing family lines, the dynasties of Erebus and Gaea demanded it, which meant he and Zephyrus should be enemies too.

A butterfly feeling quivered in his heart. Could they really change all of that? Could they create a different story for their own children and bring the city back to its former glory, back to life? He knew that he'd been drifting for too long, ignoring the hundreds of unhappy people existing far below him - the half-Gods following orders and the humans who were regularly scoured of their memories, of their liberty, of the very essence of their being. A spark of optimism ignited inside him, a feeling so new it made his palms scratchy. Stuffing a few clothes into his backpack, he took one last look out of his window at the vista below him, closed his eyes, and pressed his forehead to the cool glass.

By the Gods, let this be right; let it be the end of fear; let it do some good for all of us.

His whispered prayer misted up the pane, and as he rubbed it clean with his sleeve he noticed a wriggle of activity at the bottom of the castle, a flurry of figures whirling around the entrance doors. He couldn't remember the last time his mother had entertained visitors. Heaving his bag onto his shoulders, he glanced at the shadow clock by his bed. Ten hours into night. The hands of time were turning; he needed to make his peace with Nemesis and to send Eris her silent goodbye.

Slipping down the glass stairwells, he followed a buzz of voices and footsteps towards the Great Hall.

Steering away from the main doors, he headed for the side entrance that sat in the shadows like a crouching spider. His mettle stuck in his throat as he stood in front of the dark wood, the sound of his mother's voice spiralling out from behind it. Pressing his face to the keyhole, a thin draft of air stole the moisture from his eye and he blinked, trying to make out the blurry figures inside.

A noise sent his heart clattering against his ribs and he turned around, scraping his spine on the door handle.

"What are you doing here?" Nemesis said. "It is late and you should be in your room."

Framed by an expansive single eyebrow, her almond eyes glinted, reminding him of a wolf watching its prey. She was his mother's closest confidant, the only person who could contain Eris in a crisis. A fixer and his rock. She knew every secret and every movement of every half-God close to Eris. What did she know about him? Because he had secrets now too, didn't he? The door felt cold against his back and he knew then that he could never go back to hiding away in his bedroom or the training grounds. Zephyrus had made sure of that.

"I was looking for you," he said. "But I wanted to see my mother too. And, well I wondered what she was doing in there? Who are all the people that arrived so late to the castle?"

"Those people are... well they are... selling themselves to her."

"Are they guards?"

She sighed. "No, not guards. Do you want to go in?"

"I don't know, I don't have much time. I…I'm leaving. That's the reason I wanted to see you, so I could say goodbye."

"To say goodbye?" Her eyebrows lifted but her face remained blank. "I see."

His courage swirled away from him, leaving behind a heavy sickness. Why wasn't she surprised? Shouldn't she be saying something? Trying to stop him from going?

"I think you should look," she said. "Before you… go. I think you should know what she's planning."

The clunk of the opening door made his stomach dip and squirm.

"Go on," she said, pushing him inside. "And keep to the shadows."

Dressed in her ceremonial garb, Eris sparkled in a long, white gown with fur trim and a tall crown studded with jewels. Her luminous glass throne sat high above the room raised on a silver dais, the backrest a zigzag of diamonds that were like shards of ice. Four Red Guards flanked each of her arms, they were dressed in dark leather armour, with long black spears and spiked helmets, their eyes fixed straight ahead. Eris shifted in her seat, sending the wings of her favourite crow flapping. It hopped from the arm of the throne to her shoulder. Holding his breath, Strife tried to keep close to the walls but the glass pushed at his back. The shadow clocks sucked away another turn of the long hand and he knew he should go, that he should leave now, but his curiosity nudged him forward.

"My half-God bloodline is exemplary, Your Majesty," a tall man said, kneeling in front of Eris. He was dressed in the purple robes of Morpheus' line.

"Yes, but can you fight? Your family played little part in the revolutionary wars."

"We held a strategic responsibility, Your Majesty. We masterminded the Battle of the Five Axes. We entered the minds of the army as they slept, plotted the whole…"

"Without once getting your hands dirty?"

"Given our skills in the manipulation of dreams, we were best placed using these natural assets to infiltrate the troops."

"You are dismissed."

"But, Your Majesty, I have travelled many, many pacometers from the far south; I come with a recommendation from your great general, Tisiphone. I bring with me a token of her goodwill, a bracelet of snakeskin, taken from one of her highest-ranking soldiers."

"Tisiphone knows how much I despise her reptilian entourage and I have no use for dead flesh. I suggest you get going; you have a long journey home."

The man rose to his feet, his beard shining with oils, his cheeks decorated with black poppy tattoos.

"Hail, Queen Eris." His eyes burned with anger as he thrust his palm to his chest before stalking away with his attendants scurrying behind him.

"I fear this fiasco will only make her more enemies," Nemesis whispered, sliding up next to him.

"What is this? What is she doing?"

"She's looking for suitors," she said. "That's who all these people are. They are presenting themselves to her to become her new husband; they want to be king."

"But she's the one who got rid of my father; she will never share her power, why would she do that?"

"Necessity."

"Necessity?"

"Having another child. It's the one thing she can't do alone, she isn't just replacing your father, she's replacing you too."

Misery sank its claws into his chest. Why did he still care so much? Why did he still want her to be proud of him? He thought he'd beaten those hopes away years ago, thought he'd made his peace with the fact that he'd always disappoint her. He realised that his need for her approval still hid in the shadows of his soul, needy and sad, waiting for a small crumb of interest or affection; waiting to be loved.

"She wants a daughter, Strife."

A daughter, of course. A daughter.

Another group approached his mother's throne, wearing the green and orange robes of Moros' line. The tall man at the front had long blonde hair and a red beard. Could this be his new stepfather? Or would she get what she needed and be rid of her second husband one dark night with spells or poison, or a sharp knife?

"I have to go," Strife said. "I don't even know why

I'm here. Goodbye, Nemesis. Thank you for being there for me, thank you for looking out for me."

"Wait, listen a moment." Her hand settled on his shoulder. "I can help you if you want me to."

"Help me with what?"

"I know your friend is one of them, one of the hidden half-Gods, one of the lost children. Maybe you don't need to run, Strife. Maybe you can make your own new beginnings right here with me."

In his surprise, he pulled away from her, losing his footing and clattering into the wall. It sucked him into a cold embrace and the vibrations travelled around the hall, making the room tremble. His mother's crow turned its black eyes towards him, opened its beak in a lopsided sneer and cawed. The rest of the people in the room stared at him too, falling into silence as he struggled to free himself from the walls, kicking and punching, his panic sucking him deeper into the glass.

Nemesis took hold of his flailing limbs. "Be still, Prince Strife, you know the walls in here are as sticky as a spider's web. Be still and it will let you go."

"Get out, all of you," Eris said, standing up from her throne.

Catching a glance of pity in the cool blue eyes of the tall blonde man as the guards led him out, the compassion of this stranger left a crater in his chest and he slumped forward, dropping into Nemesis' arms.

"What are you doing in here?" Eris moved fast, grabbing hold of his shoulder, her sharp nails digging into his flesh as she glared at him, her long hair dangling in front of his face like fine white drool.

"Answer me, child!" She tightened her grip, bringing tears to his eyes. "How *dare* you spy on me?"

"I…I…"

Eris shoved him against the wall, clasping her hand around his throat, lifting him up until his eyes met hers.

"I brought him in here, Your Majesty," Nemesis said. "I was hoping to glean some information from him."

"And did you?"

"Unfortunately not, Your Majesty."

Clawing at Eris' hands, his heart slowed and his lungs screamed for air, bubbles popping in his vision. When she finally let go, he slammed to the floor, curling into a ball, choking for breath.

Nemesis bent down to help him up. "You need to trust me; it needs to look as though I'm on her side," she said in a quick whisper, reaching for his hand.

"Out of the way, Nemesis." Eris grabbed hold of the back of Strife's tunic, dragging him to his feet. "I thought you were just a harmless fool, an embarrassment, an unfortunate accident that was best ignored. But you've been sneaking around behind my back, haven't you?"

Staggering, dizziness stole his vision from him, leaving behind flashing lights and fuzzy shapes.

"I…I don't know what you mean!"

She yanked off his rucksack and threw it to the ground, the contents spilling out across the floor.

"Planning a trip, I see? Right, let's go," she said.

"Where to?"

"To the basement."

The basement was a place where screams curled out from under the doors; a place where those who entered never returned, or if they did, they came out missing limbs and the best part of their minds. He waited for Nemesis to intervene, to protect him, to *do* something, but she stood unblinking as Eris shoved him out of the door.

"Can you join us please, Nemesis," Eris said. "I might need your help."

"Of course, Your Majesty."

Dragging him to a long spiral staircase, Eris' grip was so tight he could already feel a bruise erupting under the dig of her fingers. The coiling descent and the smell of damp made his stomach dip and reel. At the bottom of the stairs a red door emerged from the gloom, lit by a flickering antique bulb, the surface giving off a dull sheen like sweating skin. Eris pulled a key from around her neck, unlocking the door which slinked open with a sigh of congested air and a stench of rotting meat. The glow of hundreds of candles illuminated a long stony-grey walkway flanked by metal cages scattered with sprouts of green mould. A black chair crouched in the centre of the nearest cell, its legs and arms were embellished with manacles and a spike of scalpels fanned out from the headrest like a horrible crown.

Red puddles decorated the floor.

A new rush of vertigo made him stumble and his

breath stuttered out in painful gasps as she swept him along the fetid corridor, through to a larger room—a square, windowless space with mud-splattered walls that were lined with rows of sharp, shining instruments. Nemesis clicked the door shut behind them and took her usual place in the shadows. He wanted to call to her, to plead for her to get him out, to help him, to protect him. As though reading his mind, she squinted at the scalpels on the wall and back at him, her look telling him that running would do neither of them any good. He closed his eyes as a wash of sickness came and went again like a squall.

Eris stood in front of him, blocking Nemesis from his view, crouching a little to look him in the eye. He returned her stare, determined not to look away, determined not to betray his fear, but as her lips curled into a hideous smile, his terror blotted everything else out.

"I won't tell anyone," he said in a whisper. "I won't tell anyone about the... the suitors."

Eris laughed, a bleak noise that matched the stuttering candles and the gloom.

"I don't give a hellhound's tooth about those idiots from the Great Hall. That's not why we're here."

"I...I don't understand."

"There's a door under your feet. I want you to open it."

One push toppled him forward onto his hands and knees and he landed with a hollow clunk on a dark circle of wood with a rusty latch. A sharp kick to the ribs doubled him over and he screamed, clutching at the pain.

"Please, Mother, I don't know what…"

"Open the cursed door, Strife. Do what I say or I'll rip off your fingers and use them to do it myself."

Fumbling for the catch, he pulled it towards him. The wood was lighter than he'd imagined, and he fell backwards, the trapdoor still in his hands. Wobbling as he tried to stand, he held it in front of him like a shield, expecting something to leap, snarling from the hole.

Eris grabbed him by the scruff of his neck and thrust his face into the pit below.

A half-God shape lay in a semicircle on the floor, his blonde hair matted with dirt, his familiar green tunic smeared with blood.

"*Zephyrus?*" he whispered.

"I see you recognise this half-God. He's a friend of yours, isn't he? I want you to bring him up here to me," Eris said.

Hesitating, he hovered on the edge of the hole.

Gods. *Gods* this was his fault! He'd left him behind; he'd left Zephyrus on his own.

"Zephyrus?" he said, his voice cracking. "Can you hear me?"

Sinking down into the shadows, he could see that his friend's clothes were ripped and purple bruises were snaking around his stomach and ribs.

"You have to get up." He touched Zephyrus' shoulder, his fingers trembling.

Zephyrus turned his head.

"Strife?"

"She's going to hurt you if you don't get up."

Zephyrus' cough turned into a wheezy laugh; his lips were smeared with blood and his front teeth were missing.

"Hurt me? Hell's Gates, Strife, she's done a pretty good job of that already."

He knew this routine, knew exactly what Zephyrus had been through, and he also knew how this ended. Hatred rushed through him like rancid water, and for the first time in his life he rejoiced in his mother's acid disapproval and he was glad that he was nothing like her; glad that he was incapable of such pointless, senseless brutality.

"Come on, lean on me," he said, crouching down so that Zephyrus could put his arms around his shoulders.

"Speed this up please, Nemesis," Eris said, circling above them.

A hand tightened around the back of his neck and Nemesis lifted them both up like errant kittens, depositing them in front of Eris, where they stood clinging to each other.

"One of my spies saw *him* in the training grounds," Eris said, pointing at Zephyrus. "Saw him pass something to you, something that looked like a note, and when he tried to follow him, he vanished. Then he turned up again at the Memory Library as if from nowhere. On top of that, this boy's memory-cleanse shows no such incident, which means he's not human at all, which means he's a half-God skulking around pretending to be someone he isn't. My crow finally caught up with him just outside the university. What are you both up to? What are you plotting?"

Stepping in front of him, she bent down so her forehead pressed against his, her eyes narrow, her breath odourless and cold.

"You have five turns of the long hand, Strife. Five turns for both of you to spill your secrets and decide your fate." She pulled a thin knife from a selection attached to the wall. "I'm going to give you this." Opening his hand, she wrapped the dagger inside his palm and closed his fingers around it. "It's time for you to prove your loyalty to me and to my crown; to decide exactly whose side you are on."

The edge of the blade reflected the red light of the room, making it look as though it was already covered in blood. An invisible hand cinched his throat shut. Zephyrus' blue eyes stared into his, and they were so clear and so brave, so everything he wished he could be. His trembling hand felt too tight around the knife, his nails digging hard into his palm.

Eris gestured to Nemesis, who nodded and followed her towards the door.

"Can Nemesis stay? Can she help me?" he asked.

"Not this time," Eris said. "This time you're on your own."

Nemesis hesitated for a moment before Eris ushered her out.

The room throbbed, its red candles dripping with

a putrid wax that filled the air with a smell like infected wounds.

"If we tell her something, anything, it will give us time," he said. "Then maybe I can find a way to get you out of here."

"I'm not giving her anything. No, Strife, my fate lies here now, in this room."

"I'm so sorry," he said, tears falling on his shaking hands. "I should have left with you as soon as you asked. I shouldn't have come back to the castle."

"You don't need to be sorry; this isn't your fault."

They huddled close together, their heads touching.

"Even if you don't talk, she'll investigate you; she has ways, she will find out who you are."

"We planned for this time; for my capture. My history has been erased and there are no records for her to trace."

"There is no way out of here, no way to escape this basement room, it is sealed with steel!"

"I know."

"So, what do we do? What do we do now?"

"What we do... what *you* do is stay very strong, stronger than you've ever had to be before. Here, take this." Zephyrus pressed a small pendant attached to a thin necklace into his palm.

"What is it?"

"It will guide my sister, Alcyone to you," Zephyrus said. "You must keep it safe. It is your time now, Strife. The next stage of this journey is yours to own, to make things right, to change history. It will not be easy; it will be long and hard, and filled with pain. But you must keep to this path; to *our* path, and to do so you'll have to remind yourself every turn of the hand of every day that it is the *right* path to follow. Please look after my sister, I think you'll be good together."

"There must be a way... there must be a way to get you out of here!"

"This isn't about me, Strife. This is about our world; about freedom and the future of our grandchildren. You can lead the army now. You can do this. You're ready."

Snatching the knife from Strife's hand, Zephyrus' fist glowed white in the gloom as he pulled the blade hard across his own neck, a ribbon of blood opening in his skin.

"No! Zephyrus! NO! Gods... GODS!"

Pressing his hands against the wound, he tried to stop the pump and slather of warm liquid. Zephyrus' fingers found his, grasping for his wrists, a terrible gurgle of wetness spilling from his mouth.

"I love you, Strife. Be strong. Wait for Alcyone, wait for my sister to come for you." He slumped forward, his head resting against Strife's heart.

"Zephyrus... Zephyrus! NO!" Sobs exploded from his chest and he hugged his friend close, breathing in the grassy smell of his hair until the metallic tang of blood swept it away. Resting his cheek on top of Zephyrus' head, he shut his eyes, wishing him Gods' speed, praying that he was going somewhere where he would see his parents again.

The sound of the door scraping open made him pull his friend's lifeless body closer to his chest.

She did this; Eris. And he *hated* her for it.

"What did he tell you? What did you learn?" Eris said.

"He told me he didn't know why he was here. He told me you were a foul witch and that he'd rather die than be tortured again!"

The back of her hand slammed into his cheek, skidding him away from Zephyrus' body.

"Well done for failing your test of loyalty. Now he's dead you are the only one left who can talk. We'll start with the scissors, shall we?" Eris' hands were shaking, her cheeks flushed, her white gown crumpled. Observing her as though from a distance, he took in her clenched fists and the permanent frown scratched across her forehead. How lonely she must be, underneath all the violence and paranoia. How sad. A weird feeling swooped through him and he realised that he felt sorry for her, for her furious anger, for the endless exhaustion of her rage. Had she ever known allegiance not brought about by terror? Had she ever loved anyone other than herself? A corkscrew of grief twisted tighter into his heart, making him hard to her; to all of it.

"Do your worst," he said. "I don't know anything."

"Majesty," Nemesis said, stepping forward and taking hold of Eris' arm. "Maybe it would be better to do this the slow way. He is upset and it will obstruct things; it will stop him from talking. I'm certain a few nights in the Pitch will loosen his tongue. Sometimes we must be patient to get what we want. Bring him back here after seven sunsets in darkness and I guarantee he'll tell you everything."

Eris brushed Nemesis off, rubbing at her temples.

"My own *son*, plotting against me."

"We were friends," he said. "How is that *plotting*? Or are you going to make caring for another person a crime now too?"

The kick to his stomach made him choke and gag.

"Majesty, I implore you to heed my counsel," Nemesis said. "You see how defiant he is? Doing this now will get you nowhere; you must remember your aim here. This is all about gaining information efficiently."

Eris paced the room, sweat glittering across her upper lip.

"I want him back here in seven sunsets, ready to talk. You better be right about this, Nemesis."

"Yes, of course," Nemesis said with a bow, slamming her hand against her chest. "Hail Queen Eris! This is the best way. The Pitch is a great leveller."

Eris grunted, "After all the privilege you've enjoyed, Strife, and all the freedom you have been given, this is how you show your gratitude? From today you will know how it feels to live without protection." She ripped his royal insignia from his tunic and threw it into the swirl of Zephyrus' blood. "Soon I will have a new heir, a daughter worthy of the throne. From today you are no longer my son."

The door wheezed open, and with a swirl of white she had gone.

"Here we are again," Nemesis said, crouching down next to him. "The two of us with a mess to clean up."

"You knew she had Zephyrus!" He jumped away from her, scuffing his back against the wall, using it as a prop to stand, clutching his bruised stomach. "Why didn't you do something? Why didn't you get him out?"

"That... situation couldn't be helped. I have no access to this basement. It's the one place I cannot go. It is a shame; he had a great lineage. He would have made a fine leader."

"How do you *know* that?"

"His similarity to his father is striking. Your mother thinks she sees everything with her spies and her truth potions, but always looking for shadows can make you blind to the things that live in the light."

Sudden tears choked him. Zephyrus the Lightbringer, what a perfect moniker that would have been for a bright new king. But Zephyrus' body was sprawled lifeless in front of him, and his own fate's path had darkened, had become invisible to him, lost in thorns and shade with the ever-watchful Nemesis as his only ally.

"So, you're sending me to the Pitch?" he said, wiping the wetness from his face. "How is that going to help anything?"

"It gives us time. You just need to get through twenty-four turns of the hand, forty-eight at most, before I get you out and then I'll have a plan. I promise."

Chapter Six

Sea Sprite

A GIANT WAVE SUCKED ALCYONE into a deep roll and she curled her feet towards her chest. She let the water close its cold fingers around her heart and wondered if the icy sea would take her away forever. But as the ocean breathed her in, taking hold of her scent and the essence of her skin, it recognised her and wrapped her in its warmest currents, swirling them around her in a safe, soothing embrace.

Welcome, Alcyone, daughter of Amphitrite; it has been too long. Welcome. Welcome home.

Home?

Was the sea her home?

The mountains were where she'd spent most of her childhood, but she'd been born in the south, near the sea, on the edge of the great desert that Tisiphone's army protected. The extreme heat there kept life simple and languid, and Tisiphone had little care for politics or what went on in the faraway capital city. This apathy meant that her parents' rebellion started there too, in a tiny coastal town, where they built their boats and their army. Their plans to finish Eris were simple— Amphitrite would captain the ships, entering Eristonia's tributaries and blocking off the trading routes, starving Eris while Asclepius led the troops on the ground. It had almost worked too, until Tisiphone stepped in and burned all their ships. Why? Because she missed the narcotics Eris traded in return for oil. The rebel boats were obstructing her supply chain and she could not feed her addiction. So, the war they had been so meticulous about planning with maps and codes and endless strategies was lost because Tisiphone needed her drugs. Zephyrus would tell this story to each of their new recruits. Be ready; be ready for anything.

On the tip of the White Plains, the ocean swirled, cold and blue and dotted with ice. When they'd arrived here, the sea had called to her and she would spend hours on the edge of the rocks, staring at the ripples, too scared to get close in case her mother's ghost dragged her away.

My 'Cyone, my sea sprite, my love.

Her memory of her mother's words, her endearments and long-faded hugs warmed her grief for a moment and she let them go, spreading them out into the current. Her mother and father were long gone, taken from her by violence and greed, but she'd not felt so close to them since she'd last seen her brother; since she'd given him his final hug goodbye. How she missed him. Her beloved Zephyrus. Her tears flowed free and fast, spinning out into the ocean like tiny silver fish.

A young guard, one of their few spies in the castle, had seen Zephyrus' body; he had helped to remove it from the basement, carrying it to one of the mass graves reserved for prisoners. Choking on his tears, he told her that he'd said the cleansing prayers, and that it didn't matter where Zephyrus' body ended up, his soul would be light of any sin; it would be free. But she didn't care about litanies, she just wanted her brother back.

Her pendant squirmed and throbbed against her throat, telling her its twin was out there somewhere in the hands of another. The pendants had been her father's last gift to them; they were filled with Gorgons' blood, which had the power to heal. An amber stone sat in the bottom of each, linking them together like magnets. Whoever had Zephyrus' pendant knew about her brother's death and she needed to locate that person, find out what happened, and take it back. She pushed away the voice telling her to lie low, to wait it out, telling her that Zephyrus would want her safe, that nothing good could come of this if Eris had the pendant. Or Strife, what about Strife…?

Had Strife betrayed them? Betrayed Zephyrus? Betrayed all they had built here in their land of ice and snow?

Five years now she'd spent in these glacial wastelands, just her and Zephyrus at first, then the others who came into their world by choice, pledging to join their fight against Eris. As their net widened, the trickle became a flow and they welcomed many more half-Gods and humans too. And so, through secret signs and hidden whispers, those innocents that were hidden in the mountains so long ago, returned to the cause of their forefathers. Is this what their parents had envisioned all along? That their children would transform into a Phoenix of war? The eldest members of their army were only sixteen, but these brave young people were loyal soldiers, intent on finishing what their parents started so many years before.

Kicking her legs, she picked up her pace, cutting through the water. She had no home, not without Zephyrus; she just had her loyal generals, her young soldiers, her grief, and her revenge. She knew these were not emotions to base decisions on, that they were not the things that kept you alive on the battlefield, but she didn't care because they were what put you there in the first place. Grief for those that were wronged, revenge on those who wronged them... and so the world turned.

Sighing, she gave into the love of the sea, letting Poseidon's invisible fingers fan through her hair, the threads of her flexible armour insulating her against the cold. Kicking upwards, she broke through the surface of the waves, reaching out towards the rocky shore, keeping a tight rhythm of movement, counting her breaths. She had travelled many miles to reach the sea, disappearing in the night, her grief too immense to share. The call of the ocean and of her mother were the only things she could hear, the only things that would help her to heal.

The sea spiralled and she felt something charge through her—a bolt of power, of energy, of something that she'd never felt before.

Take this gift; take this gift from me.

"Mother?" she said, turning in endless circles.

A whirl of water tumbled around her legs, lifting her up, out of the sea on a charging throne of spray.

The water is yours, Alcyone. Let Poseidon be your sanctuary, let him protect you.

The swell curled away as sudden as it had come, but now the ocean filled her with light. Diving deep, she swirled beneath the currents, feeling no need to rise to the surface, no need for air, and no need to leave the depths at all. Poseidon took her sadness and cleansed it, pulling it into the swell and making it a little more bearable, a little less heavy.

"Thank you," she said, whispering into the waves. "Thank you."

Amphitrite's voice had gone, but her mother's love and Poseidon's power remained with her, covering her with a protective layer as she swam for the shore, the steam from her breath billowing around her. When she waded back onto the beach, the core of this new strength, the central thread of this connection with the ocean, stayed locked in her heart. She thanked the first-God Poseidon for this forbidden gift, for the second gift she had been given. First the map of the portals and now the strength to carry on.

Her pendant wriggled against her throat, warming her neck, pulling her as it always did, towards its twin.

Closing her eyes, she wrapped her fingers around it. The time to speak to her generals would soon be coming, to put their plans into action, and galvanise their troops. But first she would make her lone pilgrimage, make her peace with Zephyrus' passing, take back the pendant their father had made for him and have her revenge.

Then she would be ready for war.

Chapter Seven
The Museum

S TRIFE SQUIRMED DEEP INTO the corner of his cell, scrunched up like a trapped insect, his legs crushed to his chest and his arms wrapped around his knees. Resting his forehead against the wall, his eyelashes scraped the bricks, blinking out the seconds as the spirits came to call. Zephyrus, with a sad smile and a gap where his throat should be; Phoebe shuffling across the dirty floor, blood stains trailing behind her; and Asclepius and Amphitrite, locked together in an endless flaming embrace. And all the others, all the countless people that he'd seen his mother torture and kill, all the horrors he'd locked away. The darkness called and they returned to him, a battalion of lost children with blame shining in their eyes.

The cell door scuffed open at random intervals, delivering tasteless meals and sometimes a fist or boot appetiser. Time had turned into something unfathomable, like a paper boat caught in waves, turning and rolling but never moving forward. His need to escape felt like a terrible itch, deep in his gut and his heart. An itch that twisted him from a shrieking blur, cursing and slamming his body at the walls, to a silent rock, his head locked between his knees. Where was Nemesis? Why hadn't she come for him? And what of Zephyrus' sister? What about her? He tried to remind himself of his promise to Zephyrus and of his determination to stay focused, to be patient, to be strong. But what did these things matter in the Pitch when he salivated every time he thought about the feel of the Sun on his skin? Sobbing, he dribbled precious water onto his knees. How long would he last in an interrogation? How long until he told Eris everything he knew just to make death come quicker, or to see one last glimmer of daylight? He clasped the pendant that Zephyrus had given him tight in his fingers, its presence his one reality, his one reminder of the outside world.

Someone shrieked from along the corridor, a terrible animal wail that set him off blinking and counting again, focusing his mind down into the detail of each scrape of every eyelash against the stones.

A sudden twitch of pressure against his shoulder made him lurch and he clamped his teeth together, biting his tongue. Swatting and clawing at the air, he clunked to the floor, his crunched-up legs hit by a nailgun of pins and needles and his mouth so dry that his scream got stuck in his throat like a blood clot.

"Shhhh, it's me. Strife, can you hear me? It's Nemesis."

"What... what are you?" His voice cracked and his mind teetered towards a deep and endless precipice. "Are you dead too? Am I?"

"I'm not dead. I've come for you, as I promised."

Something cold rested against his blistered lips and he lapped at a cascade of water, letting it soak into his parched tongue. Reaching out, he found the flesh of her arms and she took hold of him, pulling him into her chest, the familiar, sweet animal smell of her leather tunic unleashing a roll of relief, which made him retch and then sob in shoulder-heaving waves. She let him cry, keeping him close. Had she come to save him or kill him? He didn't care anymore. She had come. And that meant, one way or another, that there would be an end to this.

"Okay, Strife. We need to get going. Can you stand? Time is pressing."

"Please don't let her torture me; I'm not strong enough. I'd rather you... I'd rather you did it, now, quickly."

He leaned into her and she lifted him up by his arms, pulling his locked muscles straight. He yelped, his legs dissolving into cramps.

"I'm not here to kill you. Drink more water and eat a little something too." She wrapped his fingers around a hunk of soft bread. "Hold on to me while you walk."

"How long... how long have I been in here?"

"Six moonrises. Much longer than anticipated. I'm sorry. She's been frantic, ramping up surveillance, looking for spies, doing spot checks in the street. She had me working day and night and I couldn't get away. That means we haven't much time. The guards think I'm taking you back to the basement. We only have a few turns of the hand before she works out you're missing. You must find your strength and find it quick. I'm taking you to the museum."

"The *museum*? But it's not safe. She has eyes everywhere!"

"You don't need to stay there for long, you just need to collect something."

"Collect something? I don't understand."

"Listen to me, Strife. It is time now for focus and for action. Inside your museum, deep in its soft heart, is a jewel placed in its protection. It's something I've never been able to get close to because the museum won't let me near it… but it likes you; by Hades, it *loves* you Strife, and if you ask, it will tell you where it is, I know it will."

"A hidden jewel? Hell's Gates, Nemesis, what use is that?" As he pulled away from her, a new wave of fatigue soaked, cold into his bones. "The ghosts came, they whispered to me, but I can't remember what they said!"

Nemesis grabbed his arms. "Stop this, Strife. You must keep your head. The darkness has chewed away at you. I have some night-vision lenses. Let me give you back your sight. Hold still."

The lenses felt heavy and chalky, and as the tiny cell swirled into focus so too did Nemesis' almond eyes, her snakelike dreadlocks, and a worried crease across her forehead.

"Is that better?" she asked.

He nodded, his claustrophobia shrinking away and his valour growing back a little like a lost layer of skin.

"Now you must listen," she said, taking hold of both his hands. "The jewel that I need you to find inside the museum is a whistle, a diamond whistle encrusted with blood-red rubies forged during an age of no time in the blackest fires of Erebus' hell. A single blow on this whistle may be a silent call in this world, but in the underworld it triggers a storm, a cacophony of thunder and acid rain that awakens creatures that have been sleeping, dormant for many centuries."

"Monsters? From the underworld? By the Gods, Nemesis, how will that help us?"

"These are not monsters; they are wolves, wolves that are part of our dynasty. My own mutant gene comes from them and connects me to them. I'm hopeful I will be able to speak to them; *command* them. They are the first Wolves of Hades." She whispered their name like an incantation or a prayer. "They are our army. They are the only way we can defeat Eris."

"But there is another way. Zephyrus. There are others like him…"

"Zephyrus is of Gaea's line and we are of Erebus; our families have been sworn enemies for thousands of years. Maybe we could find peace with them, but join forces?" she shook her head. "That can never happen. Besides, Zephyrus is dead and what did he have? A handful of child soldiers hidden somewhere in the trees?"

He blinked at her, saying nothing. She didn't know about the portals; she didn't know about the White Plains.

"This army we can have right now. What better way is there to avenge Zephyrus' death but with legions of wolves that will obey us alone. Loyal soldiers who will tear your mother apart."

Tear his mother apart.

Was that what he wanted?

Zephyrus' smiled floated through the darkness, his final words surrounding him like a mist. Strength, patience, time… But where were Zephyrus' allies when he needed them? Where was his sister? The sister Zephyrus had promised would find him; would save him? His week in darkness had clarified one important thing—he had nobody else who cared about him. Just Nemesis. Letting his sadness and loneliness churn inside him, he shifted his feelings into something else, into something hard and cold.

"We can do this, the two of us," Nemesis said. "I have been waiting for so long… for the right time… waiting for you to grow; to become a man. Haven't I always been here for you, Strife?" A rare smile lit up Nemesis' eyes and he realised that the beautiful ochre splashes on her brown irises were his one constant. "With the wolves on our side, the balance of power will tip against Eris and we can win back this city."

An army; an army of wolves.

Despite the night-vision lenses, the shadows were still there; ghosts flitting in and out of corners, watching him, waiting for him. The Pitch had reopened the darkness inside his mind that Zephyrus' light had blasted away, and the black spots on his soul were multiplying like mushrooms in a damp cellar.

Squashing away the voice in his head that was telling him to be careful and cautious, he breathed more air into the blackness, setting his hatred for Eris and grief for Zephyrus free, letting it curdle like sour milk.

Nemesis was right; they needed to act now and they needed to act fast.

"Our army of wolves?"

"Yes, Strife. *Our* army."

Nodding, he took hold of her hands and smiled.

Lifting his face to the sky, he let the sunlight cascade over his skin. Closing his eyes, he sucked in every spot of warmth and followed every speckle of light that danced behind his eyes.

"Strife, are you okay?"

"I... I just need a moment."

"The Pitch reminds you to be thankful, doesn't it? To savour every second of what is good in life. To remember the smallest pleasures like the heat of the Sun on your face or the lick of blood from a fine cut of meat. Keep hold of your time in the darkness, Strife, it will make you stronger. But for now, we must hurry."

The guards in the Pitch took little notice when she bundled him out of his cell. He wondered how many of them would last the night once Eris found out they had let him leave with no more than a raise of their eyebrows.

"She's not looking for you yet," Nemesis said. "But it would be wise to keep your hood up and your head down."

The rough-woven robes she'd found him to wear were scratchy and carried the smell of neglected livestock, but they should give him anonymity for long enough to get inside the museum.

"What will you do, if I fail? What will happen to you?" he asked.

"You won't fail."

Something wriggled against his throat and his fingers found Zephyrus' pendant. It jittered against his palm, emanating a restless energy like it had something living inside it.

"What is that?"

"Oh… nothing, just a trinket… something that Zephyrus gave to me."

Nemesis stared at him, her eyes flashing in a way that made him grip it a little tighter.

"Can I look?" she asked.

Turning it in her fingers, she narrowed her eyes, her lips curled into a half-snarl.

"Has the stone inside moved at all? Or changed temperature?"

"It's just a token; it's all I have left of Zephyrus," he said shaking his head.

Her nails were too sharp against his skin and he had a sudden urge to get away. To go as far and as fast as he could. To run and run and run…

The caw of a passing crow distracted them and he tucked the necklace back inside his tunic as they hid deep inside a doorway.

"You must tell me if the pendant gets hot or cold, or does anything unusual. Can you do that?" she said in a whisper as they waited for the bird to pass.

"Of course," he said.

The lie came easy. Zephyrus had given him a gift and no matter what they were planning together he wouldn't give it up for anyone. Not even Nemesis.

"Are you still with me?" she said, taking his hands.

"Yes, I'm with you."

"Okay, then I'm going to go now. The museum doesn't like me very much. I destroyed most of its contents on your mother's orders and it has never forgiven me for it. But I'll be back for you."

"How will you find me?"

"I always find you," she said, wriggling her nose. "Your smell is distinctive. A good one, like chocolate, and it's still in there, despite the rancid robes."

A wave of sadness took hold of him and he blinked away tears.

"Be strong, Strife. You can do this."

Be strong. That's what Zephyrus had said to him too. Saying the word was easy.

"And I just ask it? I ask the museum to see the whistle and then… take it?"

"Yes, that's it. Simple." She squeezed his hand. "May the first Gods protect you."

Lowering his hood over his face, he turned towards the museum, the soft road of the Flowlands hugging his feet as he walked. The surrounding buildings were bedraggled and empty and he had little to fear from prying eyes. There were no more crows and the sky looked clear and blue.

He glanced behind him but Nemesis had gone.

Many lifetimes before Eris, when Gaea had created the city, the museum had been granted life too. It had been given its own sense of self, woven into its bricks. Gaea had meant the museum to act as a reminder, a deterrent from what went before when humans nearly destroyed the Earth, a true oracle of the past. By keeping the story of the Gods' Great Sacrifice alive she hoped that the mistakes of history would never be repeated. But as soon as Eris took the crown she removed the relics, taking away all evidence of the world Gaea had worked so hard to keep safe. Only her arrogance kept her from destroying it completely, because she wanted to fill it with her own history.

Tall Doric columns in the old style of the first Gods lined the road leading to its drooping doors. They were crumbling and leaned at awkward angles but they still gave a sense of how grand the museum had once been. The only building in the city modelled on architecture from thousands of centuries gone by, the museum was a temple, an ode to Chaos and the old Gods.

The bricks from its roof had oozed down its front like melted ice, almost sealing the doors shut, and he had to squeeze his body sideways to get through the tiny gap at the bottom. As soon as he touched the walls they glowed.

"*Welcome back, Strife! Welcome! Welcome!*"

The museum's delight at his arrival whispered into his skin.

"Thank you," he said, resting his cheek on the wall.

The surface undulated against his face and a little of its energy seeped into him, easing the exhaustion that had settled into his bones.

"*I'm sorry about Zephyrus; the crows, they followed him from here. They were too fast and I couldn't stop them.*"

"It's not your fault," he said. "I shouldn't have left him here alone."

"*It's good to see you! Welcome, Strife! Welcome! Welcome!*"

Its mantra continued like the bark of a faithful dog and he had to move his face away to quash a rising slither of shame. Before he'd discovered the training grounds, the museum had been his refuge, a cocoon of safety, a place with no judgement and of blessed silence from the noise of Eris' world. And now he was going to steal something from it.

The oval entrance hall shimmered with the toil of the hundreds of grimy human slaves used to construct Castle Discord. A series of mini galleries formed a ring around this central space, but one room called to him— a small chamber with an inverted atrium, the perfect place to hide things.

"*Have you had any visitors today?*" he said, pressing

his question into the wall through his fingertips.

"*Just you. Just you.*" The museum's answer tickled his skin.

"*Are you sure?*"

"*No visitors; just you.*"

"*What about Red Guards? Crows?*"

"*Oh, yes a crow. Patrolling the rooms. Its clacking beak makes my bricks hurt.*"

"*Where is it now?*"

"*Circling. Not far.*"

Hurrying through his mother's portrait hall, a hundred sets of blue eyes followed him as he crouched behind a door, ducking his head into his knees as a crow flapped past. Wiping a prickle of sweat from his top lip, the turquoise walls shimmered when he got up again, racing down a spiral corridor to the central heart-shaped room. The inverted glass atrium blasted sunshine inside like a torch, highlighting the prism glass statue of Eris in the middle. It stood with its right leg forward, sword raised and mouth open in a silent battle roar. As he circled it, the colours inside shifted from purple to orange to red. Crouching low, he kept the opening to the chamber in view as he pressed both hands to the wall.

"*I need your help with something.*"

"*Yes, of course.*" The museum smiled into his palms, making his shame rise again, sharp in his throat.

"*Have you got something hidden here?*"

"*Hidden?*"

"*I'd just like to see it. I know about the whistle.*"

The museum's hesitation bristled through his skin.
"Can you show it to me?"

No smile of warmth trickled out of the walls this time; just the museum's worry tingling into his hand.

"I only want to see. There's no beauty left in this world, only fakery created by my mother to bedazzle and control. It will help me to move on, help me to keep going now Zephyrus has gone."

He didn't know how well he could lie.

"Okay…You can see it; just see," the museum said with a sigh.

His victory left a chill in his heart as he pressed his thanks into the wall.

"Keep your hands there and stay still," the museum said.

A tiny black hole swirled, growing wider and wider like the porthole to a new galaxy of stars. Inside the circle, a shape formed out of the darkness, a silver smudge not much bigger than his thumb, which twisted into a glitter of jewels. Pulling it free, he turned it over in his hand, a tiny diamond whistle, encrusted with blood-red rubies twinkled from his palm.

"Gaea's children placed the whistle in my protection many dynasties ago. They wanted to keep it away from your family." The museum's nerves fluttered through the chamber like a buzz of flies.

"It's beautiful. Thank you for letting me see it."

Gods, how he wanted this treasure, how he *needed* it. The craving smothered him like a sickness.

"The whistle is deadly. It must stay here and you

shouldn't hold it for too long; you said you were only going to look."

"But, this is the key, don't you see, the way to get rid of Eris, the way to destroy her and her sisters forever." He placed his free hand on the museum's wall. *"The way to keep half-Gods and humans safe."*

"No, Strife, the wolf armies of the whistle spawn from the deepest crevices of the underworld. They do not belong in our world; they are evil, hideous horrors that can never be released."

The rubies embedded in the whistle glinted as he turned it in his hands, the blue light of the museum's walls giving the red jewels a tinge of green, like glistening spots of decay. Pride ballooned in his chest, hot and indignant. Nemesis said they could command these creatures. The museum just wanted to keep the whistle for itself.

Pressing both his palms to the wall, he shut his eyes.
"I have to take it."
"I can't let you."
"I know. I'm sorry."
He slid the whistle inside his tunic.

Before he could take a step, the floor tipped, slamming him to the ground. Crawling on his hands and knees, he moved less than a pacometer when another wave threw him into the air. Foggy heat seeped upwards and the dark shape of the crow appeared on the other side of a thin blue film that now covered the room's exit. Its sharp beak snapped as it tried to cut through.

"She killed Zephyrus, she's looking for a suitor, she is going to replace me, she wants to keep me hidden in the Pitch, most likely kill me. I need this army, I need the whistle; please let me out!"

"*I can keep you safe here, I can protect you from the crow and from her if you give it back.*"

"I…I can't!"

The museum threw Strife hard at the wall as the crow ripped into the room, its eyes locking in on him and its beak open in a triumphant cawing shriek.

Chapter Eight

Nemesis

TEARING INTO THE ROOM, the crow scratched at Strife's face, pulling a deep cut across his cheek. He batted it away with the back of his hand and it hit the floor, greasy feathers flying. Leaping behind the statue of his mother, he could feel the museum feeding staccato screams of frustration through his hopping feet.

"Give it back! Give it back! Give it back!"

The bird flew at him again, its beak sharp, pecking at his ears.

"Hell's Gates!" he roared, pulling it off his head, losing more blood to its claws as he hurled it away. The rising heat in the room licked at his exposed skin, tingling and burning. Tucking his body in close to the statue's plinth, he shifted from side to side, terrified that if he stopped moving his shoes would melt into his feet.

The crow swayed and flapped, but it didn't attack; it squawked, wings quivering as it hovered up and down. Its eyes were leaking black gunk and steam shivered off its back, filling the room with a stink like old rags.

Steadying his hands on the feet of the statue, he realised his palms were ice cold. He remembered that the effigy of his mother had been made with prism glass, a material immune to the elements, including fire. Vaulting up into its protection he wedged his foot in its elbow and rested his sore cheek against the slope of Eris' fake shoulders. The first time in his life that his mother had given him sanctuary. The museum couldn't speak to him through the prism glass, but he could still hear its screams inside the shimmer of sickening heat.

"Give it back! Give it back! Give it back!"

A sharp beak stabbed at his face, pushing him off balance. His arms freewheeled and he managed to snatch a hold with the tips of his fingers. He hugged the statue, the air in the room burning his tongue as he beat at the crow with one hand, but the stupid thing wouldn't give up, oblivious to the fact that they were both about to die.

The last rays of daylight trickled down on him and he lifted his face up to the glass roof. His time in the Pitch had made him appreciate the wonder of sunlight and at least he would die facing the day, not beaten and mad in the darkness. The sky was so close he could almost touch it; escape, just there, right in front of him, a few pacometers through the glass.

The tip of the statue's sword caught a ray of light and it glinted with a rainbow of colour, stuck in its everlasting thrust of victory. Hope fluttered high in his throat as he kicked at it, bashing and bashing with his heel. He cried out in triumph when the end snapped off, drawing the attention of the crow, which swooped at him again. As he swatted it away, its eyes rolled back in its head and it fell like a lead axe to the floor. Shimmying higher, he hammered at the roof with the sword, wobbling on his perch, the air boiling. But the roof wouldn't give.

Screaming, he held the sword with both hands, smashing and smashing.

Not a chip, not even a dent in the glass.

His blistered lips were bleeding into his mouth and his eyes were hot and sticky. The whistle's urgent desire to escape was painful now, like someone jabbing a finger in an open wound, and the museum's call didn't stop either.

"*Give it back! Give it back!*"

The bird's dying squawks added to the dig and the nag of all of them, their collective shrieks drilling through his burning skin.

"*Shut* UP!"

He threw the glass sword down at the crow, hitting the soft part of its belly. The thing flew up from the floor, entrails dangling, eyes melted into holes. It zoomed straight for his face so he had to reel backwards as it skimmed past him, hitting the roof. The white heat of its beak melted through the glass and it fizzed out into the sky leaving behind a glob of burning flesh and a hole.

A perfect round hole in the roof.

Cold air rushed in and he lifted his face up to greet the freshness, watching the edges of the glass peel away like the petals of a flower opening at dawn. The museum let out a terrible shriek as he reached up, lifting his body away from the boiling chamber, out onto the sloping glass roof.

"It will destroy you!"

The museum's words curled around his head in a blast of burning air, its sadness sticking to him, wrapping itself around his heart. But he pushed it away, letting the joy of the cool evening and the wonders of being alive lift his heels as he raced across the roof. He thought the museum would try to stop him, but its weariness seeped out of its bricks like steam and its voice fell silent.

Pulling the whistle out of his pocket, he let it sit in his palm, the rubies winking at him as it crawled around inside his head. Peeking over the edge of the roof, he could see a cluster of Red Guards patrolling the streets below.

"Where are you, Nemesis?" he whispered.

The whistle chattered to him in words he didn't understand and he clutched it tight in his hand, shivers passing through his body like a parade of dank spirits.

"Strife?"

Nemesis emerged from the shadows, her feet silent, gliding towards him. Zephyrus' dying plea telling him to be strong and patient called to him from somewhere far away. What had he done? What had he done to the museum?

"Strife? Can you hear me? Did you get it? Did you

get the whistle?"

"I've got it. The museum, I think I've hurt it. It…
it tried to kill me."

"Can you give it to me?" she said, staring at his
clenched fist, stepping closer.

Frightened now in a new kind of way, in a lonely
way that echoed the silence of his castle bedroom, he
stumbled away from her.

"The whistle… it whispers things to me."

"That's why you must give it to me; you're not
strong enough to control it," she said, her voice
soothing, like silk cloth swirling on a breeze. "Your face
is burnt. Let me help you."

Pulling a small pot of cream from an oilskin bag,
she smoothed the lotion on his blistered lips and eyelids,
the balm bringing immediate cooling relief. The whistle
had stopped its noise but he could still feel its need
pressing down like a dead weight on his chest.

"You must let it go. Keeping it will only do you
harm. I am stronger than you; I can look after it,"
Nemesis said, as though sensing his burden. A blade of
darkness shot through her eyes and there was wetness
around her mouth, making her lips shine cherry red. As
his scrambled brain stuttered, she grabbed him, digging
her nails into his skin and snatching the whistle from
his grasp. The rubies glimmered in her hand, eating up
the last of the daylight. Emptiness and longing churned
into a slam of exhaustion that made him want to lie
down and sleep.

"Finally, the time of half-Gods and humans is over

and a new era is upon us," she said, her eyes wide and round. "A time of warriors, of wolf clans and of a new history. The wolves will make this world theirs, and once you feel them, once you see how powerful they are, these new children of ours, you won't ever look back. Nothing will matter except the joy of the pack, of all your brothers and sisters running by your side."

"But the wolves... the museum said they could not be controlled. Is this right... is this the right thing to do?"

"The right thing?" She raised her eyebrows and shot him a wry smile. "You, of all people, should know by now that there is no right thing; no black or white or good or evil, only shades of mottled grey."

She lifted the whistle to her lips but it didn't make a sound as she blew. "The wolves can hear its call, but they're stuck deep underground and only blood can release them," she said. "The whistle needs untainted royal blood. It wants your blood, Strife."

Blood? Zephyrus' pendant woke again, tickling his neck. Reaching for it, he could feel its warmth pushing into his palm. Nemesis' world of moral U-turns was swallowing him up and he didn't know which fork in the path to take anymore.

"The road is set now," Nemesis said. "You must find a new kind of strength, dig deep into yourself, as I know you can. We cannot have the wolves unless we let the whistle feed."

Looking in her eyes, he could see that in her own strange way she cared for him; that one truth was in there.

"Will it hurt? I'm so tired…"

"I will control it. I will look after you."

He tried to stand up, but his time in the Pitch and his battle with the museum, the loss of the whistle and the memory of his royal insignia swirling in Zephyrus' blood, the burden of all of it had blown away the last of his strength.

"Do I have a choice?" he asked.

"What other choice is there now?"

She didn't know about the portals or the White Plains. She didn't know about the size of Zephyrus' army. Should he tell her? Should he say that there were others, that they could work with the rebels, that they didn't need the wolves? Then he remembered her words to him outside the Great Hall, telling him that the dynasties of Erebus and Gaea have always been enemies, that they could never work together. He knew that he didn't want to put Zephyrus' friends at risk, so he stayed silent.

Taking off her jacket, Nemesis wrapped it around his shoulders and propped him against a half-broken chimney.

"You are a good child, Strife. Eris doesn't deserve you. You will change everything. You will be the father of a fresh tribe. Your blood will bring a new cycle of life; a better one."

Her nails glinted as she turned his head to one side, holding the whistle to his neck.

"I've waited a lifetime for this.' A rare tear crawled down her face like a shimmering insect. "Let's wake up our army of wolves.

Chapter Nine

Pilgrimage

P ULLING HER COMPASS FROM her bag, Alcyone
aimed it due north and squinted into the
sunshine, trying hard to get her bearings. She'd
arrived in Eristonia that morning, travelling
from the White Plains and out through the portal
located in a small area of woodland close to the
University of the Eight Spires. Nocturne was the only
person she'd told about her journey. She'd made him
promise on Zephyrus' memory to keep it secret, because
she couldn't bear the thought of telling her other
generals. She couldn't cope with the arguments, with
the feet stamping and frowns as they tried to stop her.
Nocturne had been grave, but he understood; he knew
that she needed to make this journey, this pilgrimage
for Zephyrus. He promised to give her seven sunsets
before he came looking, which would be more than
enough time to find the pendant or die trying.

To keep the location of the portal safe, every trip

Zephyrus had taken into the city followed a different route. The direct trail would have been a journey of less than half a turn of the hand, but this path also risked the eyes of crows and patrols of Red Guards, and they could not jeopardise the safety of the portal. Sticking to Zephyrus' rules, she travelled around the back of the university out towards the tributaries leading to the sea. Now, tracking back inland, she realised that she had walked too far, half the day had gone by and she would soon need to find shelter for the night. Checking her map again, she traced her position using the compass and the cluster of tall trees ahead of her as markers. The Forest of Shadows. It had to be. If she walked in a straight line through the middle of the woodland, she would get to the Marshlands of Blood and Eristonia's southern trading gate in one turn of the hand. Hesitating, she traced the other routes back into the city with her finger; all of them would take much longer, another sunset at least, and she had wasted so much time already.

Resting her hand on the bag of daggers strapped to her waist, she stared at the green leaves and bronze trunks of the forest. It didn't look as ominous as she'd feared. Zephyrus had warned her of the things that lurked there, the creatures that survived on the blood in the soil, fed by the marshlands, things that would do anything for a taste of fresh meat.

Maybe she should take the longer path.

The pendant burned, its urgency growing. Alcyone weighed up her options again—half a turn's walk through the trees or another long trek and overnight camp in unknown territory. Stuffing the compass and map in her bag, she took a deep breath. Decision made; she would take her chances with the forest.

Pulling a trader's cloak from her backpack, she tucked the musty material around her shoulders, hoping that the disguise would make her less conspicuous. Head down, she pressed forward into the trees, the green canopy blocking out the remaining light, immersing her in the gloom. Claustrophobia wriggled in her belly as the darkness inked into every corner. Pushing her bad feelings away, she concentrated on the weight of the throwing knives clanking against her hip.

"HIYAAKK."

The sharp noise prickled at her neck.

"HIYAARKKK! HIYAARKKKK!"

Creepers tiptoed along her spine and she stopped at the next tree, gripping the bark as the forest filled with whispers. The feel and smell of the wood settled her nerves a little and she took in slow breaths, telling herself to stay calm, that noises couldn't hurt her, and if she could just keep moving she would soon be out in open land. But her fingers were frozen to the tree and she could feel a presence, a sense growing all around her that she had unwanted company. Forcing herself to take a step away from the tree, keeping her arms straight out in front of her, she plodded on. The darkness was so thick now she couldn't see her hands. The sounds were growing louder, like an off-note, cold and unnatural.

A thin green-tinged beam smoked across the forest

floor, helping to light her way, helping her to speed faster and deeper into the trees. It formed a path and she followed it, desperate to get out, not really thinking where it had come from or where it would lead her. Something cold brushed across the back of her hand and terror swallowed her senses. She stumbled, tripping over gnarled roots, branches snatching at her hair, a force yanking at the chords of her spine and a shadow clipping her heels, pulling her down.

It's just my shadow, it can't hurt me.

But what of the things Zephyrus had told her about? The things that lived in the forest, the things that liked to feed on clean souls.

Scrambling forward on her hands and knees, she gulped back tears, heading for the thin curve of yellow brightness just beyond the gloom. A cold force ripped at her again and her face hit the floor, filling her mouth with mulch. Sobbing, she dragged herself on by her elbows; her legs were a dead weight and a shadow sneaked up on her, drowning her in darkness. She grit her teeth, her arms were burning but her anger boiled stronger than her fear and it kept her moving. She didn't want to die here, not at the very start of her first real quest.

The pendant of Gorgons' blood lifted from her neck, blasting like a torch, the blood and amber stone inside it shining an orange light over her body. A shadow hissed, slithering away from her, morphing into human form. A trickle of feeling returned to her muscles and she crawled faster, the thing trailing behind her. More identical black shapes were sliding across the forest, slinking closer and closer.

"Keep away from me!" she yelled at them. "Keep back!"

The light of the pendant picked up the glow of sharp teeth and white faces circled by black hoods. Vryloakas—blood-drinking undead, dozens of them, swarming all around her. She'd never really believed they existed, and had thought they were the stuff of ghost stories told by firelight to wide-eyed children.

With a collective hiss, they lifted their heads towards her, a hundred red eyes, staring.

"Drop the pendant."

"Come to us."

"We will keep you warm."

"Don't be scared."

Their voices filled her head, soothing her. Her arm grew heavy, the pendant dropping into her neck.

"That's it, join us."

"We will love you forever."

"We can feel your sadness."

"We're all orphans here."

Dark corners beckoned to her, inviting her to explore their blissful solitude. As the creatures spoke she could feel her grief for Zephyrus fading and the tight band around her heart loosen. The shapes opened their arms as she rose to her feet, gliding away from escape, back into the forest.

It would be good to rest, to sleep, to be peaceful. Closing her eyes, she leaned against one of the trees.

"Yes, that's it, you can slumber with us."

"We will help you forget everything…"

The creature nearest to her smiled, nodding its ugly head.

Soupy thoughts turned sluggishly around in her mind and she struggled to connect any of them together. The figure edged closer, flashing sharp yellow teeth. It rested its hand on the back of her head, pushing it down so her pendant slinked from her neck, dropping to the floor.

"You don't need that here," it said. "You don't need *anything* here."

The vryloakas' fingers were like shards of healing ice, numbing her sadness with the promise of eternity. Telling her that she too could become a shadow in the darkness, an empty vessel, with no fears, no sadness, just the love of the night and a hunger for other people's souls. Letting the creature take hold of her, she snatched a breath of the cold, empty home it would make for her. A home with no grief, but with no love either. Despite the temptation of it, of the wonderful bliss of forgetting, she realised that having nothing, *being* nothing would be worse. It would be far, far worse than the raw rub of her pain. She didn't want to give up her self or her memories, not now, not for a long time.

She wanted to live.

Scooping up the pendant, she ran, hurling herself around trees, reaching out for the scrap of sunlight in the distance.

A vryloakas leapt on her like a cat, clinging to her

shoulder, its drooling lips searching for her neck. She slashed at it with her dagger, tearing out a chunk of its greasy hair, which wrapped itself around her hand like a snake before she flicked it off. Stabbing at it again, her knife found its leg and the thing dropped away, snapping with frustration.

"Stay with us…"

"NO! I'm stronger than this, I'm stronger than you!"

Racing towards the open country beyond the darkness, she threw herself out of the trees, skidding across the wet scrubland on her stomach. Something caught at her foot and she screamed, rolling over, a dagger in each hand, her legs yanked into her chest. A dark tongue flashed from the trees but the final rays of sunlight sizzled its tip, sending it hissing back into the forest.

Pushing into the soft earth with her heels, she shunted backwards until her spine hit a prickly bush. Her heart hammering against her ribs, she scraped wetness from her cheeks with the back of her fists. She wouldn't give up, no matter what this land threw at her. She would keep her mind fierce and clean, just like she'd taught Zephyrus, so long ago, when they'd first found the White Plains.

My twin, my twin, my twin…

The pendant whispered to her, waking from its trance, remembering its other half, hidden somewhere in Eris' city.

Brushing off dead leaves and smears of red mud, she

staggered to her feet, turning away from the trees to focus on the journey ahead. The black shapes in the gloom were still watching her and she could feel the throb of their irritation as she stalked away. Weaving through alleyways of green tundra, she stepped around the pools of bubbling quick-mud. The Marshlands of Blood were left over from the old world, from long before Eris' time. The old songs told that the marshlands were a monument to the sacrifice of the first Gods and that the blood in the soil came from their veins. The overgrown path twisted uphill, and she followed it, climbing higher until it opened to a view that took her by surprise, glueing her to the spot. Eristonia sparkled below her, Castle Discord blasting up from the blue foundations of the Flowlands. It reflected so many colours she couldn't put a name to half of them.

She'd never imagined that the city would be so beautiful.

As she stared, the pendant jabbed and wriggled.

"What is it?" she said, grabbing hold of the glass.

Over there, over there, over there.

It pulled on her neck until she faced to the west, towards a large cube of blue sitting on the edge of the Flowlands. The pendant skipped next to her skin and she frowned.

"The museum?" her words danced the pendant into a buzzing frenzy. "You want to go there?"

My twin, my twin, my twin...

Had Zephyrus hidden his pendant in the *museum*? Could it be that easy? She hesitated; this didn't feel right somehow, but she knew she must follow its call. So, she strode on, down through the boggy shrubs towards the city walls.

The trading gates were quiet and she held her breath as the guard examined her fake papers before nodding her through. The blue citadel looked like an upside-down ocean, the road pulling at her feet, creating tiny waves as she walked. Only a few other people crossed her path, most of them keeping their heads low, avoiding eye contact. A trio of crows hurtled overhead, their beaks clattering.

Quickening her pace, she visualised the map in her head. The roads of the city were set out in decreasing rectangles and she knew she would pass through seven streets on her journey from the southern gate to the museum.

My twin, my twin, my twin.

The pendant whispered its lullaby as she walked.

Drawing closer to the museum, she spotted a quiver of red hovering in front of its doors and goosebumps prickled her arms. Two Red Guards were circling. Waiting until they disappeared around the side of the building, she ran closer, crouching behind a glass bench. The guards were patrolling the circumference of the museum and she wondered if they had been posted there because of Zephyrus. Had they followed him from the museum to the university? Did they know he'd been here? Should she turn back? Worry niggled at the base of her spine and her feet longed to run, but the pendant thrummed against her throat, reminding her that she should follow its lead, and that… well… she had nowhere else to go.

Sighing, she waited for the guards to appear again and then she started to count.

One… two… three…

A crow skimmed its wings along the road in front of her, leaving a mini valley in the soft turquoise.

Sixty-two… sixty-three…

The guards glided past the entrance and continued with their patrol.

Sixty counts, she had sixty counts to get in the door. She remembered what Zephyrus had taught her about Red Guards, about the strength of their armour and the speed of their fire-swords.

Her stomach sliding, she hesitated, doing the count again.

Sixty-one this time.

The guards disappeared and she ran, pumping her arms, counting down in her head. The squashy road sucked at her feet, slowing her down, but when she pushed the door it nudged open without protest.

No!

The pendant tugged, sharp on the back of her neck, digging hard into the skin. *Up!*

Up? Shaking her head, and confused, sickness crawled like beetles in her stomach. She'd stopped her count at twenty and now she had no idea how much time she had left before the guards reappeared.

My twin, my twin, my twin!

The pendant twisted and pulled.

Up! Up! Up!

"By Poseidon!"

Glancing up at the doors, she could see that the facade drooped with small, melted sections and she jumped, reaching for one of the bumps and missing it.

How long did she have left? Ten counts? Five?

Fumbling with the bag around her waist, she grabbed a knife. She slammed it as high as she could into the door with the back of her fist and pulled her foot onto one of the nubs.

A blast of hot air sizzled her toes. The guards were hovering underneath her, they'd stopped marching and were hissing to one another in a language she didn't understand. Closing her eyes, she pressed her body into the door, sweat flowering in the palms of her hands. She didn't want to be tortured, she didn't want to die, not yet, not now. The muscles in her arms were burning and she nudged her toes across the door, desperate to find a hold, but she reached too far and both her feet slipped away from her. Dangling from her cramped fingers, she lost her grip, her bottled-up breath escaping in a whoosh as she fell. Closing her eyes, she sent a prayer to Poseidon. Whatever happened, she would fight back; she wouldn't let anyone take her to Eris' basement.

The museum sighed a long whistle of air that flurried around her like the elegant flutter of a butterfly's wings, and as it did the door's angle shifted to take her weight. It lifted her up across its surface away from the threat of the guards below.

"Thank you," she said. "Thank you!"

"*You have the first Gods' protection, daughter of Amphitrite, but this isn't for them, this is for Zephyrus' memory,*" the museum whispered. "*And for Strife. He is making a mistake and he needs you, he needs your help.*"

Strife? Her heart quickened. What did it know about Strife? She waited for something more, but the museum stayed silent as it lifted her up onto the roof. Lying still as the pendant fluttered against her throat, she waited for the burn of a fire-sword against her skin, but nothing came. When she looked down, the guards had gone. Crouching low, she moved slowly across the roof, her knives tight in her fists until a movement ahead threw her back to the ground. She could see a shape, a person, shoved against a chimney and wrapped in leather like a rolled-up rug. And a woman, crouching in front of the figure and whispering, her long, matted dreadlocks dancing in the wind.

Sliding behind a broken pile of bricks, she watched the woman stand up and pace. She had a ragged natural beauty. A scraggy mountain cat in human shape. The woman threw her arms wide, gesticulating as the body in front of her wriggled. Narrowing her eyes, Alcyone took in the angle and distance, knowing they were close enough for her to get a clear shot with her daggers.

But not yet.

Her pendant buzzed with heat, which meant one of these people had Zephyrus' pendant, and if she killed them now then her questions would die with them too.

The bundle moved, and a head appeared from

underneath the leather.

Wild curls and a young face—the face of a teenage boy.

The boy reached for something shiny that the woman held in her hand, something that glinted with jewels. The woman snatched it away, leaning down again, holding him by his shoulders.

The boy's dark skin glowed, beautiful against the blue of the roof.

The woman raised her hand and slashed it down, cutting open the boy's throat and shoving the shining object under the cascade of blood. The thing slurped at the wound, and as it drank, it shrieked—a gloating, hideous SHREEEEEE of noise that crawled inside her ears and under her skin. It shrilled over the rooftop and it sounded like the vryloakas, but her heart told her this was worse, that the noise inhabited something base and feral that thrived in the deepest sludge of Erebus' darkness. The figure of a person shimmered in and out of focus like a ghost, a hideous hunched creature with its sharp teeth buried in the boy's neck. A symphony of howls rolled towards her, sticking to the wind as this thing drained its victim's blood.

Then she saw something else catch the light—a silver chain around the boy's neck smeared with gore, and a pendant. Zephyrus' pendant.

The boy screamed, his wide terrified eyes the colour of summer violets.

Violet eyes.

Strife; it had to be.

And the dreadlocked woman must be the queen's

half-sister, Nemesis, her right-hand woman, her spy and the descendant of wolves.

Its job done, the hunched creature faded away and the small, shiny object plinked to the ground.

Nemesis pressed her hands to Strife's neck.

"Strife; Strife! You must stay with me!" Nemesis wrapped a length of cloth around the wound on his throat, breathing into his mouth and thumping at his chest as his face turned white and his lips changed from red to blue.

"By the Gods!" Nemesis shouted at the sky, tears dripping from her cheeks, her fists pressed tight to her sides. "I didn't want to kill him!"

Hugging him close, she kissed the top of his head, closing her eyes and whispering a prayer before leaping off the side of the roof.

Alcyone blinked, feeling numb as she watched the pool of blood growing thicker and wider.

What had she seen? By Poseidon, *what* had she just seen?

The pendant drummed at her skin and the museum nudged at her heels, forcing her to stumble forward. Kneeling next to Strife, she stared at his grey skin and open, empty eyes. He looked so young; this boy who had caused so much trouble and who Zephyrus had loved so much. Exploring his throat, her fingers were sticky with blood when she finally found the silver pendant and yanked it from his cold neck.

Chapter Ten
Wolves

A PAIR OF GREEN eyes flickered at him from out of the darkness, the colour mesmerising, like dappled sunlight shining through leaves. Smiling, Strife wondered if these eyes would lead him somewhere good, somewhere new, somewhere better. Then, as his mind cleared, he remembered. He remembered the whistle and its call. He remembered the beast with teeth like straws, stealing his blood. He remembered the distant howls and his life fading away from him. And Nemesis' tears; he remembered Nemesis' tears most of all. And as he phased in and out of consciousness, he thought he heard Zephyrus' voice, calling to him, telling him he needed to fix things, and that he needed to stay strong.

The green eyes stayed with him too, waiting and watching.

Rolling over, he clenched his teeth, ready for the pain and for whatever gaping wound the beast of the whistle had left him with. But his body felt strong; in fact, it felt good. Frowning, he put his hand to his neck; his fingers searching for ragged flesh or scabs of blood, but the skin there was fresh and smooth.

"Am I a ghost?" he said, whispering into the darkness.

"Not yet."

The voice startled him and he jumped, scratching at the floor with his heels.

"Who is it? Who's there?"

A girl sat cross-legged on a high rock platform that jutted from the mud walls of a windowless room. The bright light gleaming from a torch had turned her long curls into a shock of fire and her green eyes were narrow, scrutinising him. He'd never met her before, but there was something familiar in the shape of her face and the sprinkle of freckles across her nose.

A dagger glinted from each of her hands.

"What happened to Zephyrus?" she said. "Did you kill him? Did you spill our secrets? What does your mother know?"

The questions were like slaps, and he blinked, surprise sending him mute.

I love you, Strife. Be strong. Wait for Alcyone, wait for my sister to come for you.

Zephyrus' words. Words he'd chosen to forget about.

"Why was he captured? *Who did you tell?*"

Alcyone. Despite him, despite *everything*, here she was, just like his friend had promised.

"Answer me!"

"My… my mother," he said, his words coming in a rush, "she captured him. One of her spies saw him pass me a note in the training grounds and she must have tracked him down. She had him in the basement. Gods, she tried to get him to talk but he is… was strong. He… slit his own throat to keep your secrets safe… I think Eris wanted me to do it, but I couldn't; I couldn't kill my best friend!"

Swift as a cat, she leapt off the ledge, leaning over him, pressing her knives into his chest.

"Your *best friend*? He asked for your help, he risked his life to see you, to get you away and you *left him alone*! Did she see the portal? Does she know about the portal?"

The blades were pressing hard into his tunic. He shook his head. "No… I don't know! I don't think so. I didn't know he'd been followed from the museum. I thought he would go back to you, I thought he would go home!"

"He should never have left me, but I couldn't make him stay. His stupid belief that you had some courage, that you could help us. That's what killed him. YOU killed him!"

Staring into her eyes, he soaked up their anger and their grief, and a wash of calm tumbled over him. He relaxed into the blades. She deserved vengeance for her brother and maybe if that meant a knife in his heart, so be it.

"No. You are not giving up. I'm not going to let it be this easy for you!"

126

Pushing him away, she slashed her knives into the walls, cutting and stabbing into dirt and rock, huge tears magnifying the freckles on her nose. After a while, her blades clanked to the floor and he watched like an idiot as she sobbed into her hands.

"I'm so sorry," he said.

She shook her head, sending water flying. "You don't get to be sorry! I should have left you up there on the roof to die. Why did I bother to heal you? What a cursed waste of the last of our Gorgons' blood."

Heal him?

As his fingers searched again for the wound that should have been bloody and painful on his throat, he realised that Zephyrus' gift to him had gone.

"Zephyrus gave me something, a necklace, a pendant!" Dropping to the floor, he scraped his fingers through the dust, searching for it. "It's gone! Can you help me find it? It must be here somewhere, it has to be!"

A look of surprise glanced over her face and he could see how little she trusted him, that she really didn't believe that he'd cared for Zephyrus at all. Tears dripped on the back of his hands as he scratched around in the dirt.

"Stop it!" she said, looming over him.

He flinched as she yanked him up by the arm.

"I've got it! *I've* got Zephyrus' pendant." She lifted two necklaces from her throat, dangling them in front of him. They were an exact match; twins, clinging to one another like magnets to metal.

"These pendants were the last gift our father gave

127

to us. They are linked, and will always be drawn together no matter how many miles there are between them. My pendant brought me to the roof of the museum; to you."

His hand hovered near his throat, remembering how the necklace had pulled him forward, how it had wanted to find something. By the Gods, that was why Zephyrus had told him to be patient, he knew the pendants would bring them together. Why hadn't he listened?

"Gorgons' blood has another property," she said glaring at him. "It can bring souls back from the very edge of death. Which is exactly where you were up there on that roof."

"You used it to save me?"

"Yes, I saved you, because of Zephyrus; because he would have wanted me to."

Misery pressed into his chest, closing around his heart like a vice. The roof. The whistle. Nemesis.

"I need to tell you what happened on the roof, I need to tell you... what I've done."

"Yes, you do."

Something rumbled under their feet, the ground shifting.

"Where are we? What is this room?" he said.

"A cellar in one of the houses near the museum. I couldn't get far; I had to carry you. You were barely conscious and very heavy."

"Did you see anyone else?"

"No, the guards disappeared when Nemesis did

and there was a flurry of crows, but they were moving fast, a swarm of them, heading for the castle."

The sound came again like a distant roll of thunder, convulsing through the ground, harder this time, slamming them into the wall.

"Gods, we need to get out!" He grabbed her hand and she tried to pull away, but the vibrations were so strong that she had to cling to him to keep upright.

The floor churned, bubbling dirt up into the room, followed by a long brown snout with yellow teeth which snorted and wriggled. The thing thrashed, falling forward with a growl, gasping for air. It coughed up an enormous lump of earth, spitting it across the room before standing, shakily, on four legs. The wolf panted, its eyes glowing orange in the half-light. His breath wedged in his throat as another one twisted from the ground, snapping and howling as it laboured out of the soil. The two wolves grunted, turning in circles, sniffing at each other.

He could feel them. He could feel their thoughts, feel the force of them tugging at his skin and through the pull of his blood which coursed through their veins too. And their hunger, the terrible pain of their hunger; he could feel that most of all, like a white-hot spear in his stomach. The first wolf, the largest, blinked at him, its tongue hanging long from its jaws.

Nodding, it seemed to acknowledge him as one of them, as if he too were a wolf.

Because they were made of his blood, they were his children.

Sate hunger. Find pack.

Hunger. Pack. Hunger. Pack.

The wolf's red eyes slid away from his and focused in on Alcyone.

"She's mine," he said, "leave her alone."

The wolves took him in, their muzzles pulled back into matching snarls, assessing his position and his power.

"Step back," he said, "find the pack, leave us, leave us alone."

They bowed their heads but their newborn hunger screamed louder than his tentative command.

The lead wolf howled, leaping towards them, its jaws wide, pinning him to the floor. Scrambling for a grip on its fur, his fingers were useless, sliding off grey bristles thick with buried earth. As they wrestled, the second wolf went for Alcyone, its jaws circling her arm. Screaming, she crunched a dagger between its eyes and it yelped, landing hard, knocking the first wolf from his chest, spinning them both into the wall. It snarled into his face, its rotting animal breath making his eyes stream before it collapsed on top of him. Yanking the dagger from its face, he shoved it off, turning to catch the other one before it could find its feet, planting the knife into the back of its neck.

The release of their souls felt like a sharp hook, grabbing at him, trying to take him too as they disappeared back to hell. The soupy stink of dead wolf covered the inside of his throat like a film of oil and the full strength of the pack bayed for their loss. They called to him to stop this and to join them. Pushing them away, their murderous howls and the terrible need of them, he forced the noise into a murmur that he could contain. For now.

"What *are* they?" Alcyone said, gripping her bleeding arm, wobbling a little.

"Wolves. The whistle…"

"Will there be more? Where did they come from?"

"From hell… they come from hell."

"From *hell*?' She shivered, her face wrinkling with pain. "By Poseidon, Strife, what did you do?"

Leaning against the wall, his heart floated high in his chest, pushing against his ribs, making it painful to breathe.

"They came from the whistle. That thing that took my blood on the roof lives inside it; the whistle called them."

He closed his eyes tightly and told her everything.

"Gods Strife, *Gods*. What a mess, what a terrible, terrible mess!"

His confession left him hollow; he thought he'd feel better, but he didn't. He felt grubby and wrong like the hidden bruise on a shiny apple.

"Nemesis wants the same as we do, she wants to get rid of my mother," he said.

"By filling the world with *wolves*?"

"I don't know… I… I don't know."

"Why didn't you leave with Zephyrus when he

asked, when he risked… when he gave his life to come back for you?"

"I know what you must think of my mother, of Nemesis, of my life, but they are my family. I needed a little bit of time to see Eris and to say goodbye to Nemesis. She loves me in her own way, I know she does."

"She just killed you!"

"She didn't mean to."

"Nemesis knew that the whistle needed your blood but she didn't warn you, did she? She just took what she wanted and she ran."

"I saw her tears, I saw her crying…"

"Do you know how you sound? These women… they are poison."

"I didn't know what else to do. I didn't know that the pendants would find each other. I didn't think you'd come."

A starfish of wrinkles crinkled her forehead and she lifted her eyes to the ceiling, huffing out a long slow breath.

"Zephyrus loved you, he believed in you, despite everything, despite me pleading with him to leave you, to forget about you and to stay with me. You should have trusted him as he trusted you."

An unexpected spike of anger jabbed at him. It filled him with bitterness. She hadn't spent years watching people die in the worst ways possible, she hadn't spent endless hours with the ghosts of these bodies haunting her in the Pitch. What did she know about his life? What did she know about being let down? What did she know about the many painful failings of trust?

"Maybe it's best that you just go," he said. 'You should go back to your portal and your White Plains before any more of those things spawn from under our feet."

"I can't go back, not yet. This wound… my arm. I can't risk exposing our soldiers to any kind of disease."

They stood in silence, her eyes sparking with life, the emerald shine calling to him, muddling with the whisper of the wolfpack inside his mind and forcing his anger back into its stagnant corner. Did he really want her to go? Did he really want to be left alone?

"I need help to wrap this up," she said, nodding at her arm which she cradled to her chest. "There are rolls of hessian inside my backpack, can you get them?"

Fumbling with her bag, he found a pouch with some roughspun bandages and a small bottle of clear liquid.

"Is this it? Do you have tinctures for the pain? Any herbs for infection?"

"Those things are scarce. We smuggle in what we can but we don't use them freely. We have been saving them, stockpiling ready for the possibility of war, ready for when we take the city back from Eris. There's no need for a fuss; the alcohol will help to clean off the worst of it."

A ragged gash decorated the meatiest part of her forearm and he doused it with the liquid, wrapping it in the bandage as tightly as he could.

"I can help you to get more medical supplies," he said. "My mother has all types of herbs stored in the University of the Eight Spires. And, well, I am tied to you now. The ancient stories say that if your life is saved by another, your soul hides inside theirs forever."

"Old wives' tales," she said with a snort.

"Let me… let me do this… to repay you for giving me back my life."

A stink of musty fur clogged the airless room and Alcyone's eyes were planted towards her feet, her good hand locked into a fist. He wanted to tell her how much he'd loved Zephyrus and that he would try to be here now, here for her too. Instead he stood, awkward and useless, staring at the dead wolves lying in the shape of a cross on the floor, praying to whatever Gods of goodness that were left in the world beyond that she would let him help her.

"Okay," she said looking up to meet his eyes for a moment. "I don't have a lot of choice, do I?"

"I suppose not," he said. "I'm glad I can do… something."

"You had better take one of these then," she said, holding out a knife to him, "to protect yourself."

"Thank you."

The floor shifted again, and they glanced at each other, lifting their daggers, ready for a fight. But the jaws of the earth churned inward this time, hugging the dead wolves into a muddy embrace, swallowing them back underground.

"It seems that they don't belong here, even in

death," Alcyone said. "Shall we go?"

Edging their way out into the silent streets, they were greeted by the first light of dawn. Sticking close together, they ran towards the central residences, skirting around mounds of mud that had broken through the road.

"What's happened to the wolves?" Alcyone asked.

"They don't like the sunshine; they'll be hiding in darkness waiting for night to fall."

"How do you know that?"

"I can hear them."

"Can they speak our language?"

"No, I don't think so, it's my blood. They are mine; of me. I can understand their thoughts."

"Can you give them commands?" she said, stopping and taking his arm. "Can you speak to them too?"

"I don't know. Their voices are more like a feeling than a sound. I'd need to work at it, but maybe…"

Shadows flew across her face and he waited for her to say more, but she kept silent, turning back to the road. His heart hollowed as he trudged along next to her, the whisper of the wolves catching at his thoughts despite his attempts to nudge them away. He wanted to talk to her, to plead for her counsel, to ask her what in the name of the first Gods he should do now, but how could he ask such things when she wouldn't even look at him.

The buildings around them were dark, their blue bricks a deeper shade of raspberry purple. At first, he thought the colour change was an illusion created by the sunlight, but when he walked closer to examine the walls he saw the blood. Great swoops of it sprayed across every building, across the square, across the front of the Memory Library, acres of red liquid that looked as though it had been poured from the sky. Alcyone spotted it too, and she ran her finger across a window, staring at the mess on her skin with wide eyes.

"Where are all the bodies?" she asked.

Hunger. Hunger. Hunger; deep in our bones, threaded in the roots of our souls.

"They need to eat. They have a terrible hunger, I'm not sure there's anything of the bodies left."

"Oh," she said, blinking, "oh."

She stared at him as she wiped the blood from her finger across her tunic. "What's to become of the city, Strife? What's to become of humans and half-Gods with these killers prowling the streets night after night?"

"I don't know."

"That's not good enough. You did this and now you need to fix it."

"I need time to work out what to do…"

"We don't have any time." She turned away from him to call down the empty street. "Is anyone here? We can help you. Is there anyone still here?"

"What are you doing?" he said. "We need to keep quiet!"

"If there is anyone left alive I can help them. They can go to the portal in the forest. I will take them through with me to the White Plains."

"It's too risky to make so much noise! We are under Eris' watch."

"And what else do you suggest we do? Leave them as wolf food? I might be a half-God but I am proud of my humanity, aren't you?"

A small face appeared at the crack of a nearby door and a large pair of brown eyes blinked at them.

"I see you!" Alcyone said, running and pressing her hands against the door. "Please, whoever is in there, please listen to me. You can't stay here! You have to leave the city."

"Go away!" said a gruff female voice. "Leave us alone!"

"I stand here with, Strife, heir to the crown," she said, glaring at him as he tried to protest. "This chaos will only get worse, you must leave, take as many others with you as you can. Go to the woodlands next to the university. I will come and find you, I know a safe place. I can take you there."

The apartment door slid open. "Did you say Prince *Strife*?"

"Yes. I am Strife. And she's right, you must listen to her, you must go," he said.

"What is this new hell brought upon us by half-Gods? These creatures, these *beasts*, what are these things? Why doesn't the queen protect us?"

A small girl with big black eyes and brown curls peered out from behind her mother's legs.

"Are you a real prince?" she said. "Do you have a crown?"

"Shhhh, Cassandra, enough!"

"You cannot stay here," he said. "Once the Sun sets they will be back for you."

The woman stared at him, her eyes were red, and pink sores decorated her mouth where she'd been rubbing at the skin.

"Please," he said, "for your children."

"Let go of me and find your sisters," she said, shooing Cassandra away, pausing to glare at him. "We have to pack, we have a journey to make."

"Travel by day only," Alcyone said. "Take a weapon, go to the forest by the university and if I am not there when darkness falls… hide."

The woman nodded, closing her door.

Moving on through the streets, they called and searched, giving their message to all those who had managed to hide. As the hours of the day ticked away, he could feel the pack's hunger growing again. In just one night they had wiped out most of the families in the central apartments, how long would it take to kill everyone in the city? Thirty sunsets? Less?

Nemesis didn't tell me about their hunger, she didn't tell me…

"I need to rest for a moment," Alcyone said, leaning against a wall, her face flushed.

"Can I look at your arm?"

Closing her eyes, she nodded, letting him pull back her sleeve. The makeshift bandage seeped with fresh blood.

"Are you feverish? Do you feel sick?"

"No, I'm okay. Tired that's all."

"It's time to find you that medicine,' he said. "If we move fast we'll be at the university in less than a turn of the hand."

"Okay," she said. "We've done the best we can here."

As they headed out of the city centre, he could see a fuzz of red circling Castle Discord. Eris had clustered the force of her guards around her fortress, safeguarding herself, leaving her citizens alone with no protection, leaving them to die. A lone crow tailed them for a while until Alcyone sent it spiralling into the road with a dagger through its neck.

A sudden flash of heat sliced across his chest and he lurched to one side, a Red Guard circled them, swirling its flaming sword. He slashed at it with his dagger and it staggered, unsteady, looking as though it had been in a fight already, its armour dirty and ripped. It lurched for him again as a knife thudded into the back of its head. He had to skit to the side to stop it falling on him. Alcyone nodded at him as she pulled her blade free.

"Two of them!" he said, and she frowned, not understanding.

A flicker of movement in the shadows, a sparkle of magenta, zooming quickly. It reached for Alcyone's hair but he got there first, pushing her out of the way, grabbing it by the neck and pulling his knife across its throat, he let the body slide onto the floor, his heart thumping.

"They always work in twos," he said. "It's something to remember… for next time."

"Good to know," she said with a curt nod, dusting herself off.

They had the potential to fight well together, to work on their synergy, to become a practised team. And he wanted to say it, to tell her how fluid they could be as soldiers; how natural. But he didn't have the courage to say the words.

They plodded on in silence, skirting the castle, heading out to the eastern gates. A splash of blood adorned the glass windows of the empty sentry post but the gates were still locked and they had to climb up the wall. Swinging his leg over the top, he could see one of the university's metal spires glinting in the distance.

A sadness wriggled inside him. Once they had the herbs, Alcyone would be gone and he would be alone again.

Except for the wolves and their howling inside his head.

"What's that over there," she said, pointing towards a dark warehouse tucked into the hillside like a scab.

"The Pitch," he said, "that's the Pitch."

As they picked their way down the wall, he couldn't stop thinking about the hundreds of prisoners stuck inside the Pitch. Would the guards be in there too? He doubted it. They were selfish cowards who would have fled at the first wolf's growl. His skin felt too tight against his bones. There were so many of them in there, so many helpless, broken people with no light and no food.

"I can see the university," she said. Its eight imposing turrets, each a different coloured metal, were catching at the rays of the Sun, shining brightly, shooting light up into the sky. "It's so close, a quarter of a turn at most."

"I… I have to go to the Pitch," he said.

"The *Pitch*?"

"Whatever's left of the people inside, I need to get them out."

Chapter Eleven

The Pitch

ALCYONE STARED AT HIM, shaking her head, pointing to the sinking Sun.

"We can't go to the Pitch. We've only a few turns of the hand before night falls!"

"I'll be fast… and the prisoners, they all hate Eris. They can use your portal too, they can be healed and trained to fight."

"Emaciated flash addicts as *soldiers*?"

"Most of them were good people once, good people whose lives were taken away from them because they didn't comply with the rules, or because my mother didn't like the look of them or the line of their family tree."

Just like Phoebe; poor dead Phoebe, beaten and assassinated in a filthy cell.

"You were talking about keeping hold of our humanity, right?" he said.

She nodded, her nostrils flared and her lips pressed

tightly together.

"These people need our help," he said. "And if we leave them in there to die we're no better than my mother."

Their eyes locked and he held on to the intensity of her scrutiny, allowing her to dig into him, trying to get her to see that he wanted to make up for what he'd done.

"By *the Gods*!"

Leaping off the gate, dust exploded from under her feet and her curls flew out behind her as she stomped off towards the Pitch.

"I'll take that as a yes, then." He sprinted to catch up.

They skirted along the outer line of the city wall, the university's spires disappearing behind them.

The Pitch loomed like a black hulk of misery, and as they slowed and got closer to the front gates, his neck prickled, expecting an ambush. The doors were half-open and the scorpions and snakes decorating them winked at him as they scurried through. A swirl of smoke curled up from inside the courtyard. One of the torches had been ripped off the walls, starting a fire that had destroyed a wooden shelter next to the inner gates. The bodies of guards were scattered like fallen leaves across the square. Kneeling next to one of them, Strife started rifling through pockets.

"Check that one in the corner, look in his bag for keys, and we need night-vision lenses too," he said.

"Why are there bodies? I thought the wolves ate what they killed."

Burning; burning Sun; shadows, shadows…

Their voices were faint but there, always there.

"They do. But the Sun must have been rising. These guards were killed in haste, so the wolves could get inside the Pitch and escape the daylight."

Finding a cluster of jangling metal clasped in a dead fist, he pulled the keys free, pushing away the guard's lifeless fingers with a shiver.

"Shouldn't we bury them or at least cover them up?" she said, hovering near one of the dead guards. His arm had been chewed off at the shoulder and his chest was ripped open. The wound buzzed with flies.

"There isn't time."

"It won't take long," she said. "Now you can at least help me pull them into the shade."

They heaped the tangle of limbs together in the lee of the wall and Alcyone mumbled one of the old prayers as they stood in front of the pile of broken flesh. He had known some of these guards, known their cruelty, their stupidity, and their neglect. Peeking at Alcyone, he watched her raise her fist to her forehead in the mark of respect that came from Gaea's line, not his own. He didn't feel much for these people, but he understood the fine line that separated him from them and how easy it might be to become a monster too. So, he closed his eyes and sent off his own prayer to whoever might be listening, asking for something different, for something better; chanting it over and over until Alcyone interrupted him with the touch of her hand.

Attacking the inner gates, he scratched endless

wrong keys into the lock, cursing, his fingers fumbling. When the doors finally creaked open, he had to take a step back. A hot animal smell swilled out, the air thick with it, with *them*.

"Gods," Alcyone said, covering her nose with her sleeve. "That stink, you can almost touch it... like maggots and... latrines."

"It's the perfect place for them to hide," he said.

"So, there are hundreds of starving beasts inside and we are still going in?"

Glancing up at the Sun, he assessed its position in the sky.

"Yes, we're going in. We've got two turns of the hand before dusk. Let's aim to be done in one. We will be gone before they wake up."

An outhouse for the guards squatted on the other side of the courtyard. The place where new prisoners were stripped, showered and given their uniforms, and the last place they would see daylight. A spike of heat sizzled down his spine. The darkness and the ghosts from his own time in the Pitch were etched into his mind and he felt sick at the thought of going back inside. But he pushed his fear aside, his need to help escalating into a scratchy obsession. He had to save the people trapped in the darkness; he *had* to. Raiding the hut, they grabbed canteens of water and a stash of night-vision lenses before pushing open the thick, leaden gates into total darkness.

"*Strife?*"

A new voice whispered in his head, a singular voice,

rising above the pack.

"*Strife? Is that you?*"

"Alcyone? Did you say something?"

"No," she said, staring at him. "Are you okay? Your face looks sort of weird."

"I… I'm fine," he said. "Let's keep moving."

"*Strife? Can you answer me? Are you there? Are you alive?*"

Nemesis. It was Nemesis' voice.

By the Gods, she'd found him because she had somehow become part of the pack too; part of *his* pack.

Propelling her out of his head, he focused back on this mission, on the Pitch and the prisoners and on getting some of them out alive.

Nemesis would have to wait.

They tiptoed along the high walkway that led to the cells, their feet creaking over hundreds of wolves that lay together like question marks in the exercise circle below. He could feel the drift of their nightmares and their cycle of rising hunger. Could they feel him too? Shivering, he blanked them out, just like he did every time his mother beat him, dissolving his thoughts and memories into liquid; into nothing.

Grubby faces were pressed against the bars of the first cells, the stink of their unwashed bodies mingling with the fug of the wolves. At the sound of their approaching footsteps, the prisoners banged on the metal rails, crying out for water.

"Shhhh!" he said. "You must be quiet!"

"We heard howls… and screams." A boy at the

front reached his fingers through the bars and grabbed hold of Strife's elbow. "We haven't had food or drink for more than a day."

"Here, take this and pass it back," Alcyone said, pressing a water flagon through the bars. The boy grappled for the top too quickly, spilling half of it before he could get it to his mouth.

"Water! Water!"

Tentacles of arms snatched at them as they pulled the full supply of canteens from their bags.

"More! We need more water!"

"How are we going to get them out of here? Look at them," she said, stepping back from the scratch of clawing fingers. "They are half-starved and their brains have been deadened by the darkness."

A fight broke out. Two twigs in rags wrestled for a flask. The winner didn't have the power to hold on to her prize, she dropped it and then lapped at the splash of water on the floor like an animal.

"Even if we can get them out, will they have the strength to find the forest and hide before dark?"

"I don't know, but we're still going to try," he said. "The Pitch, the blackness, it does terrible things to you, but once you get out, once you see the world again… you can heal. I'm sure some can be saved. It's worth it just for that, isn't it? With the wolves ripping through the city we can't afford to waste even one life. You said the same thing to me. Back in the Flowlands."

"Okay," she said. "I'm with you. Let's get this done."

"Thank you."

Then she smiled at him, properly smiled, her face lifting, her eyes sparkling, making his heart sing and then catch with pain... because once she got her medicine she would be gone.

"Right,' she said, walking in front of the bars. "You all need to take three steps back and stand still, hands by your sides; can you do that?" She banged on the metal with a dagger. "Three steps back! Now!"

The anemone of bodies retreated into the gloom.

"Prisoners with tunics numbered 108, 56 and 809, can you step forward? You will be the eyes of your cellmates. I'm picking you because you look strong. Are you strong, can you lead a group out of here?"

"Yes," a young woman with large watery blue eyes and a shaved head answered. "I can do it."

"What about you? 56? 108?"

"Yes!" the two men replied in unison.

"Good, now you three are my Lieutenants, and my Lieutenants do not answer to numbers. What are your Gods given names?"

"Helene, mistress."

"Arion," said the man.

"Doros." A younger boy with brown hair nodded from the darkness.

"Here, we have lenses for you, do you know how to use them?"

A new crush of limbs wriggled like spiders through the bars, trying to grab hold of the lenses, scratching and clawing.

"Step back!" His voice sounded too loud around the chamber and he could feel the wolves stir and roll in their sleep. "Step back from her, she's trying to help, she's trying to get you out alive. Do you understand?"

Someone hissed, triggering a mumble of dissent, but they all moved apart to let Helene, Arion, and Doros through.

"We will do our best to control them," Helene said, taking her lenses with a bowed head. "The dark, it peels away your layers, takes away your self-respect."

"I understand, Helene, but we do not have time for frailty; the turn of the hand is against us," Alcyone said. "Listen! All of you! You must form three lines with Helene, Arion, and Doros at the front. They will be your eyes. Keep hold of each other's hands and move in a chain along the walkway. You *must* be quiet; there are wolves asleep in the exercise yard and they will be right underneath your feet."

"Wolves?" a smaller girl said, a sob catching in her throat. "What wolves, miss? Why are there wolves?"

"They are Nemesis' army," he said. "We are in a state of civil war. She is using them to… to defeat Eris, but they are difficult to control; they are hungry and violent. We need to get you away from the city. We know a place of safety; a refuge. Head to the forest near the university and wait there for us. Cover yourselves with mud, the soil will mask your scent from the wolves."

"We are weak," Arion said. "Some of the older prisoners haven't seen daylight for decades. And the flash addicts… you know what the vials do to them. I don't even know if their eyes will be able to cope with real light."

"You have no choice," Alcyone said. "If you don't leave, you are certain to die. I'm opening the gates now, so keep hold of one another, keep hold and keep moving."

"No choice?" her words echoed through and around the prisoners and as the cell doors creaked open they hesitated, shivering.

"Hurry! Hurry!"

The first line shuffled forward, but they were slow, their bare feet stumbling.

"They need to move faster," Alcyone whispered. "We have already been in here for too long, the Sun will soon be tipping back towards night."

Moving up and down the lines, they collected up the stragglers, cajoling and nudging them as they crept onto the high walkway, moving far too slowly over the heads of the restless wolves. A metronome in his head ticked away the time. He'd underestimated how many people he would need to go back for, to shunt and encourage, to half-carry or to drag sobbing out of their cells. Some of them had been in the dark for so many years that they were terrified of leaving. Alcyone followed his lead, carrying the youngest, leading the oldest. And while they fluttered around like nursemaids, the buzz of the pack grew louder as hundreds of hungry monsters rose from their nightmares.

"They are waking up, Alcyone," he said, grabbing her arm. "We have to get out!"

A single scream filled the darkness.

And then a howl. A long, piercing howl.

Organised lines tumbled into chaos and Alcyone disappeared away from him, swirling into the mess of bodies. The first cluster of prisoners poured out into the shimmer of daylight and he prayed that they remembered to run and run fast. Turning away from escape, he searched for her, calling and calling.

"Alcyone!" Where are you?"

"Here; here!"

After all her protests about helping, she had kept her place at the back of the line, still trying to herd the weakest of them towards the light.

"We have to go. Now!"

Grasping for her hand, he pulled her close to him and they ran together, the shrieks of the prisoners tumbling over them. The wolves were snatching at limbs, gulping down bits of bodies in swift, sickening chomps. They stabbed and slashed their way through but another wolf seemed to appear before a dead one hit the ground. Hordes of confused and sightless inmates were going the wrong way, dredging them deeper into the Pitch. They raced away from escape, the wolves picking off the prisoners behind them until just the two of them were left running alone. They squeezed through the barred metal doors that they'd just run from, slamming the gates shut behind them.

"Maybe we can just stay here, until they sleep

again, until daylight?"

The terror in her eyes made him want to scream and cry and bang at the bars, but he stamped it away, taking hold of her hands.

"I hope the ones at the front make it... I hope some of them get away. This is my fault; I'm sorry you're in here, I'm sorry you came with me."

"Stop it, Strife. We did the right thing. We did the *right* thing."

Teeth and claws appeared from the darkness, galloping towards them and grinding into the bars; hundreds of powerful bodies that raged with their need for food.

"*Strife.*"

"*Come to me, Strife. Come to me.*"

"*Where are you? Strife? Strife?*"

Nemesis' voice. Growing louder and stronger; pulling at him. He shoved it away but it was getting harder, her connection to him not just coming from the pack but from their family line and their history.

Leave him.

Leave him.

Nemesis' voice smoked through his head and a small group of the wolves stepped back but the rest ignored her, not recognising her commands.

By the Gods, she didn't have them, Nemesis hadn't secured control.

Nobody had.

This pack had no lead voice and no master.

They growled as they pressed into the metal, their

eyes the same colour as the ruby red stones of the whistle that had called them into life.

"They're going to break the gates!" Alcyone said.

"We have to keep going."

They sped towards the centre of the prison, into the inner bowels of the Pitch, past the smaller locked cell, that had almost lost him his mind what felt like a lifetime ago. Alcyone's touch helped him drive the pack's voice away and he kept a tight hold of her hand as they flew through the darkness. He knew that whatever happened he would do all he could to protect her. Another huge metal door loomed up in front of them and he fumbled with his set of stolen keys as the thunder of weighty claws grew louder and louder.

"Hurry, Strife, you must hurry!"

One of the keys turned in the lock but the door would not budge. As they heaved and pushed, he slipped, circling away from Alcyone across the floor.

Hunger. Pack. Hunger. Pack.

The endless mantra rolled on and on…

Leave me alone!

He thrust his voice through the pack and the wolf in front snarled and yelped, shaking its head and pulling back, giving him the gap in time that he needed to sink a knife into its neck. A splash of blood arced across his face as he yanked it free and the beast thudded to the floor. He kicked it away, adrenaline pushing him to Alcyone. Two of them were circling around her, forcing her into a corner, taking it slowly, ducking and snapping. They were learning, getting a feel for her moves, keeping track of the pattern of her previous kills from the voices of their brothers and sisters. They were smart. Smarter than he'd realised. He crept up on one of them, sticking his foot under its back legs, sending it spiralling across the floor, giving Alcyone the window she needed to stab the second one in the chest.

As he fought, he lifted his mind, elevating it, as he always did in the training grounds into to a wider perspective, assessing every inch of the corridor, every item, every scratch, every stain, looking for weapons, for a different way out, for anything that might help them.

Walls, bricks, metal floor...

And a switch. One large switch high up on the wall.

Using the back of one of the wolves as a springboard, he jumped into the air, grabbing Alcyone and lifting her with him as he slammed down the lever. A lake of fire crackled across the floor, lighting up the darkness with an intense blue light, sending the stream of oncoming wolves into a sizzling dance. His arms were burning, pain ripping across his chest from the weight of them both, only managing five counts before letting go. The river of fire disappeared back into the walls as they dropped onto the hot floor.

"What was *that*?"

"Prisoner control. Come on!"

Yanking at the door, they squeezed through the gap and dragged it closed behind them, securing it shut with bolts. The small room was covered in rusty taps and levers, and large clanking metal pipes criss-crossed the ceiling. They pressed and pushed and turned everything they could see, searching for a way out, but nothing opened. Nothing moved.

Sinking to his knees, he pressed his hands into the side of his head, trying to think, trying to keep strong. How long until the wolves broke through this door too? Even if they managed to keep them out, how would they survive? They had no food and they had given their water to the prisoners. And what about Nemesis? Could she save them? Could she stop the wolves?

Closing his eyes, he opened his mind up to the roar of the pack, searching for Nemesis within them.

"*Nemesis?*"

"*Strife? Strife? Help me!*"

The full force of her call slammed his head against the wall, sending blood trickling down the back of his throat.

She didn't have the power to help him, not when she didn't have the pack under her control.

"Strife! Strife!" Alcyone said, shaking him. "Are you okay?"

"Yes... yes," he said, blinking up at her.

"Stay there, I'm going to look at the pipes." She lifted herself into the nest of metal with her good arm, the bandage on her wound covered in dirt and specks of blood. Resting her ear against the tubes, she tapped at them, listening, her nose wrinkled.

"These are water pipes, I think it's the main supply for the prison!" she said, her eyes glittering.

He shook his head, not understanding.

"The pipes will lead out to a water source. If we follow them, if we swim through, they are our exit. They are our escape."

Chapter Twelve
Pipes

"GO THROUGH THE PIPES?" A twisting feeling squirmed through his stomach, up to his throat. "When I was a child, my mother… if I'd been bad, she would put me in a bath and… I can't. I can't put my head under water."

The door shuddered, the metal vibrating, buckling inwards.

"I am not your mother, Strife. Whatever she did in the past, you must let go of it. All you'll need to do is hold your breath and I'll do the rest." Her palm felt cool and her fingers firm as they closed around his, and the touch of her skin numbed his fear a little. "I have a gift given to me by Poseidon. I have an affinity with the water. It will make this easy and it will help you too. You just need to hold on to me, keep your arms flat, take a big breath and don't let go."

A gift? From Poseidon? That kind of thing had

been forbidden by Chaos when their new world came to life many centuries ago. Immortals interfering with humans had caused too many problems in the past. The first Gods were not permitted to give powers to anyone.

"The world is changing and we are in crisis," she said as though reading his thoughts. "Chaos turned his back on us a long time ago and Poseidon loved my mother. Do you think Chaos cares that he is helping me? Do you think he even knows? And my grief… my grief for my parents and for Zephyrus, that's what made him do it, it was an act of kindness. He felt my pain, and he wanted to wash it away."

Yes, their world had shifted, but first Gods intervening like they used to? What kind of world could that bring? But as she stared at him he knew that he had no right to judge her, not after everything he'd done.

"Okay," he said, "you're right, I… I trust you."

She nodded at him, squeezing his hand then letting him go.

"First we need to open up the pipe. I can prize off the bolts with my knife, then we'll use our weight to stamp on it, to force it open."

As she climbed up into the metal, he scraped around the floor, trying to be useful, trying to search for something to help her. Nails and screws were spilling from an abandoned tool bag, and when he shook it upside down a river of silver streamed to the floor. Scooping through it, he pulled out a small iron hammer. Sliding up through the network of pipes, he handed it to Alcyone. The last few bolts wouldn't shift and she cursed, bashing and bashing, the thump of her cudgel matching the explosive beat of his heart.

A noise froze them and they both turned towards it. A fissure, like the crack in an eggshell, snaked down the middle of the door, and as they stared it widened into a scraggle of claws wriggling through the gap.

"Come on; come on!" Alcyone screamed at the pipe and he jumped up next to her, the thick metal jarring his knees. With a creak and a groan, the pipe snapped, pouring water into the room.

"This is it, Strife! Hold on tight!"

Her curls swirled up around her, the water lifting and turning them into red seaweed as she held out her hands to him.

A finger of panic pressed into the soft dip in his throat. What if the tunnel was too small to fit inside. What if it was hundreds of pacometers long… What if…

As he hesitated, a bolt from the door came shooting past his nose and a mass of wolves skidded over the water, their haunches flattened and muzzles pulled into hideous sneers. He sucked in a last ragged breath as Alcyone wrapped her arms around him and pulled him into the pipe.

A wriggle of nerves churned in his belly; memories of his mother forcing him into a bath of ice water, shoving his head under again and again, choking and suffocating him. He counted the seconds as they twisted through the tube, corkscrewing, faster and faster. His arms were locked around Alcyone's chest and the force of her power flowed through her skin, melting into his, feeding him courage as they went spinning into a whirling tornado of speed. But as the turn of the hand ticked by, his lungs seared with white-hot pain and the old panic took over, shrieking to get out, his body screaming for air. Water filled his mouth, the liquid strangling him with an intense suffocating agony that slowly faded into a heavy feeling of letting go that lifted his consciousness up into a sphere of healing light…

A punch of cold air smashed the bubble into shards of pain and he retched up streams of slime as Alcyone held him tightly, circling him in her arms. After a while, his tremors stopped but neither of them tried to move; they lay next to each other, staring out at the water. They were crouching on the banks of a reservoir, the lake sparkling with the light of the rising Moon.

"You're okay and we're out; we're safe, we're safe," Alcyone said, whispering the words over and over.

A shiver set his teeth rattling, and cold convulsions twitched through his limbs.

"You're in shock. We need to get inside and find somewhere warm," she said.

A small ramshackle outbuilding crouched behind them, leading to a higher watchtower. He lay on the ground as she scurried up a wooden ladder into the shack, coughing again and again until the pain in his lungs finally subsided from knives to needles.

"All clear," she said, clattering back down to him. "Do you think you can walk?"

He nodded, letting her help him, his knees shaking

as they climbed the steps.

The pack had fallen quiet in his mind for now, the voices far away, his exhaustion overpowering their noise.

The watchtower had a circular view spanning the reservoir and the city beyond. They could see hundreds of black shapes bleeding toward his mother's castle in a dark river, collecting recruits on the way, newly birthed creatures spilling out of craters of earth.

"How do we fight them?" Alcyone said. "How do we get rid of an army that spawns fresh soldiers on each rising Moon?"

"I… I don't know," he said.

But maybe he did know. Nemesis' call; the panic in her voice. She needed him.

The bandage from Alcyone's arm had gone, swept away by the water, and the wound looked red and irritated.

"We need to get you the healing herbs. We are close to the university," he said. "We can be there in less than half a turn of the hand."

"We need to keep hidden until dawn and we need rest. The water, it's helped me a little, it'll keep me going for a while," she said.

"This gift, your power, Poseidon's rule breaking… I've never heard of it happening, not since the days before the Great Sacrifice."

"My mother's ghost or her spirit, she persuaded him to do it, she forced his hand."

He thought about his father and how long he'd

searched for him. Why hadn't his father found him? If Amphitrite's spirit was strong enough to help her daughter with her grief; to call on one of the first Gods to use his powers, then why hadn't Kratos heard his pain too?

"Look over there, Strife," she said, rushing to the window. "Look at the gates!"

A thin thread of people weaved in a line away from the city. As they stared out at the straggle of refugees, his shoulder brushed against hers and she didn't move away.

"I… I'll never forget… what you did and what happened… what happened to Zephyrus," she said, not looking at him, her nose pressed to the glass. "But I can try… to forgive."

Swallowing down a flash of tears, he leaned his head against hers.

"Thank you… I… that means a lot. Thank you."

They stayed that way for a while, watching the evacuees from the Pitch, willing them onwards, willing them to safety.

"There are supplies here, food and water. Let's eat and rest and then I think it's time for you to start your training," she said.

"Training?"

"It's time you learned how to get your body through the portal."

Closing his eyes, he let his arms fall to his sides, focusing on the darkness inside his head and trying his best to quash the flashes of panic fizzing like fireworks in his stomach.

"You have to keep your mind empty, let your thoughts drift away. Let your fears and emotions go free, and fill the space left behind with a person or a place that you love, that is part of you, that you want to see with every fibre of your being," Alcyone said.

"Zephyrus," he said. "I'll think about Zephyrus."

"You then need to merge your mind and your body. It feels like a magnet, circulating its force into your blood, forming millions of connections, countless particles of yourself each with their own bolt which will fuse you into the portal."

"How will I know if I'm doing it right?"

"It starts with terrible emptiness, like you're about to lose your whole self, like an endless drop, a falling sensation, then, well it hurts a little bit, but you get used to that after a while."

Breathing deeply, he let a fuzzy picture of Zephyrus form behind his eyes. Zephyrus in a ruffled green tunic, strong and steady, like a young tree growing tall in a field of dust. Standing in front of him inside the armoury. But as he concentrated, nothing happened and Zephyrus' face drifted away again.

"I don't feel anything," he said. "And if I try to think too hard I can't keep my focus."

"You're letting your mind click in but not your body. It's a different connection altogether. Try again, but when you think of Zephyrus, imagine your body attaching too, get him to give you something to hold."

Opening and closing his hands, he tried again, taking his diamond blade sword from Zephyrus in his head, feeling the hilt against his palm, turning it so the green jewels sparkled.

"Take the mind-bolt deep into your blood, your bones…"

Pulling into the throb of the pulse in his neck, into the shunt of his own blood, he started the fission in his palm, with his sword. And when he found it, the floor floated away from him, melting him, so he had no substance. The weight of his body sent him hurtling into the nothing and he could feel this nothing joining with the sword, to his mind, and into the core of his beating heart.

Then a million spikes of pain shot up his arm and along his spine like glass speeding through his blood.

"*WHAT ARE YOU DOING? WHERE ARE YOU? STRIFE? STRIFE!*"

Nemesis' screams ripped him out of the nothing, back into the round room of the watchtower and Alcyone's constant gaze.

"You were nearly there," she said.

"The pain." He sat on the floor, his head dizzy, a film of sweat covering his skin. "I… the pain…"

And Nemesis' voice, clearer than it had ever been, beaming into his wide-open mind. He knew then that he couldn't enter the portal. If he did, Nemesis would find him and so would the pack. He couldn't risk that happening and that meant he could never travel to the

White Plains, not until all the wolves were dead.

"You learn to ride it, like a wave; it only lasts a few seconds. It's just the shock, of hitting it for the first time," she said. "If we'd been at the portal, you would have been through."

"I think I just need to rest for now," he said.

He curled up on the floor and his body felt hollow; a husk of exhaustion, but his brain hopped and jumped like a rabbit on a hot road. He had to tell her, he had to tell her about Nemesis. But if he did would she just go? Would she leave him and forget about him forever?

"Tell me about the mountains where your parents hid you," he blurted, wanting her to talk, wanting to hear her voice. "Where did you go when you were small?"

"On the cusp of Alecto's territory in the far north, outside the reaches of Discordia, hundreds of pacometers from civilisation," she said, sitting cross-legged on the table in front of the window, staring out at the water; keeping watch.

"Alecto? Gods, she's worse than my mother; barely human. What about her bats? Don't they hunt up there?"

"There are caves with underground tunnels, vast and unexplored, they go deep into the mountains. Too deep even for the bats to nest inside."

"Were you alone there?"

"There were other children for a while and we had guardians, forest archers, who brought us supplies and trained us how to find our own food. Once the wars started, our parents couldn't risk coming to see us. We were still so small... but we had each other; we always had each other..."

The tears on her cheeks sparkled like diamonds.

"Zephyrus managed to find a friend in the caves," she said. "He made a pet of one of the bats, a runt that had been left to die by its mother. I told him it was dangerous, that the thing couldn't be trusted, that it would turn on him; on me... but he didn't listen... and he loved that ugly thing, even when it grew to be the same size as him. He used to scratch its scraggy ears and feed it rats and it followed him everywhere." She paused, turning to face him. "It loved him too and it died protecting him... protecting him against one of its own kind."

"I miss him so much," he said, hoping she believed him. "He taught me how to use my throwing knives and he found me my courage. I don't know how I'll be able to fight all this without him here."

Her lips quivered and she pulled her hands into fists, her hair a mess of damp curls, her face flushed. She looked beautiful, like a sad pure-blood Goddess.

"When Zephyrus decided to claim you, Strife, to train you and love you, he knew he could die. He knew the risks and the dangers. I want him here too, the Gods know I do, but Zephyrus is gone, so you must stop; stop thinking you're not good enough; stop thinking that this moment, this present should in some way be different. When that bat fought for Zephyrus, killing three larger creatures with the power of its love, it was majestic; it soared like a dragon and gave everything it had… but in the end, it just wasn't strong enough… whereas you, Strife, you are not a runt. You can't let your history eat you away, you must give more, you must *be* more; more than yourself, more than Zephyrus, more than anything you ever thought you could be because *you* are the future. You are a king."

Words scratched at his throat, wanting to cry out, to deny what she said, to tell her that he wasn't worthy of Zephyrus, or of her. Words that wanted to share how his insides festered with a terror greater than he'd ever felt before, that a swooping fall of sickness threatened to floor him every time he heard the pack calling, that he had no clue what to do or to say, and that most of all he just wanted to get away from all this, to run and run and never look back. But he stayed silent because of the set of her jaw and the determined way she scraped away the tears from her cheeks; because he knew he had to stop tarnishing Zephyrus' memory with his own cowardice and his guilt… and, well, because she knew, she knew it all already because she saw it every time she looked in his eyes.

Chapter Thirteen
University

COILED TOGETHER ON THE hard floor, they got very little rest. The sounds of screams and howls carried to them across the water on a feral wind. Nightmares chased Alcyone's sudden fever and he cooled her forehead with water as she tossed and turned, calling out for Zephyrus. The wound on her arm was swollen and tinges of yellow infection dotted the jagged red bite mark.

All through the night he listened, hovering a little closer to the noise of the pack, picking up on the chaos of their movements, hearing Nemesis fighting for control. He knew what he had to do, knew that this would be his last night with Alcyone. Sorrow weighed heavy like a stone in his chest. Why did their paths have to divide just as they were finding their peace with one another? He wondered if he had been cursed, whether happiness would always be out of his reach. The turn of the hand moved slowly, the sludge of night sticking to him. Hugging her shivering body close, he willed her to keep fighting for just a few more hours.

At first light, he half carried her out of the watchtower. Their movements were slow, skirting around the reservoir through the scrubby tundra beyond the city walls to the university. Once inside, they found the complicated citadel of staircases and asymmetrical rooms that twisted up into the university's eight towers, each of them made from different metals, their colours swirling together like layers of lava.

"It's beautiful," Alcyone said. A mist of sweat had flattened her hair to her forehead and her lips were pressed together in a grey line.

"It is," he said, letting her rest and catch her breath. "Almost there."

They scaled the stairwell that spiralled through the Copper Tower. The metal walls were expanding with the Sun's warmth and they clinked and clanked around them as they climbed. Before his mother's rule, each of the turrets of copper, aluminium, silver, bronze, iron, steel, chromium, and gold had represented different seats of learning, the melding metals of the hallways reflecting collaboration between disciplines. But that had been many moonrises ago and his mother had thrown anyone with a sniff of academia about them into the Pitch. So, the university stayed empty, a wasted place of wonder, just like the museum.

A tall, thin door glimmered from the top of the staircase and he thumped at it with his fist, the sound reverberating around the walls.

"No security," he said. "The guards must have been called back to the castle."

"Or they've run away."

"I don't think the Red Guards *can* run away, they're not like the guards in the Pitch, they're not really human or half-God. They don't have any free will. They're like machines. I think Eris is making sure all her guards are protecting her and her castle."

"Abandoning everyone else to their fate," she said.

"Yes," he said. "At least her selfishness makes her predictable. Now we just need to find a way to get in this room."

"That's easy. Inside my backpack is a metal spike, can you get it?"

He nodded, pulling out the long needle and handing it to her.

"Nocturne taught me this," she said, wobbling a little as she threaded it into the lock. "He's one of my most trusted advisors and my first human general. First of many, I hope. I need you to take your dagger and slide it quickly down the gap when I tell you to," she said. "Ready?"

He nodded.

"Now."

A smile drifted across her face as the door clicked open.

"That's a great trick," he said. "How long has Nocturne been with you?"

"Many, many sunsets. He's been watching over you too, for a long time, long before Zephyrus made his pilgrimage to the city," she said. "He's the whole reason Zephyrus came to find you. Nocturne lost his family during the revolutionary wars. His brother was killed fighting in your mother's name and his wife and children died of starvation. He sacrificed everything for Eris and she rewarded him with contempt. He was demoted to armoury keeper; his military position replaced by the Red Guards. A great warrior left to clean training swords. He'd been loyal to your mother all his life."

"She cares little for anyone but herself," he said.

"Well, Nocturne learned the hard way that there's no reward for humans in Eris' regime," she said. "All the darkness in his life should have made him bitter but it hasn't. He said that you had something of your father in you, but your mother has spent her life trying to beat it out of you."

"He said that?"

"He did. He persuaded Zephyrus to come here to find out what you could do and then to train you up."

She shivered, catching hold of his arm to steady herself.

"Did Nocturne know my father? He never said anything to me."

"Yes, Nocturne fought under Kratos' command for many years before he disappeared. Nocturne thought that Kratos had questioned Eris' methods, that he hadn't wanted to go to war, that he'd wanted to meet with my parents, to work out a truce. He wondered if Eris banished him or made him disappear somehow. He was never convinced she would take responsibility for killing him, he thinks Kratos is the only person your mother has ever really loved."

"I don't know, Alcyone, she has no loyalty."

"Maybe not, but she respects great warriors, doesn't she?"

"Perhaps," he said, "but she's never hesitated in killing anyone before."

"I need to tell you something," she said. "The map of the portals appeared next to my bed one night when we were living in the mountains. We never knew who gave it to us. But it used to… sing to me, a song of chains in the wind, of metal and battle and swooping swords. Nocturne is sure it has something to do with your father, that Kratos left it for me."

He stared at her, the crease of pain inside his heart forcing him to blink away tears. If his father *had* helped Alcyone and Zephyrus why didn't he help him too? Why didn't he come to the city and rescue his only son?

"Where is the map? Could I hear the song too?"

"We destroyed it, holding on to it was far too dangerous," she said. "I'm sorry, Strife, we don't know for sure if there is a link and I never saw him, I never saw anyone."

She rested against the open door and closed her eyes.

"Are you okay?"

"You might have to help me, I'm not sure if I can walk."

"Wait there just for a moment, I'll check that it's

safe first," he said, ducking inside.

His mind churned in the dim silence of the dark room. Could his father still be alive? He'd stopped believing, stopped even hoping so long ago it hurt to think about it. And it had never even crossed his mind that Eris might think of her own son as a threat too. Was that why she beat him? To make sure that he never had a chance to shine? To keep her female bloodline clean of men, with no possibility of protest from her abused, downtrodden son?

Together we are one. Together we must feed.

The wolves' sleeping breaths still buzzed around him like white noise.

"Can I come in," Alcyone said, peering around the door. "Is it safe?"

"Yes," he said. "Come on, let's find the healing herbs. But be careful, half of these supplies are poisons. Here, put this on just in case." He tugged a mask from the wall and pulled it over her head then grabbed one for himself, the metal and cloth mesh moulding to the shape of his nose and mouth. The smell reminded him of the basement and its rusty stink of death.

As he grew accustomed to the dark, the rows of labelled glass bottles wobbled out of the gloom. Glancing along the shelves, he recognised his mother's scrawl.

Cholera-pox poison: fast acting. Death in less than a sunrise.

Malarial flu: doesn't cause death in all cases. Needs work.

Gods.

His foot brushed against something and he jumped back as a bottle rolled under his foot, wobbled, and lay still. Sweat prickled at the back of his neck as he leaned over to scoop it up. He read the label before he placed it next to the others on the shelf.

Rabies: hallucinations; dehydration; hydrophobia. Death is slow but certain.

He knew all about rabies, he'd witnessed its effects first-hand on one of Eris' human lab-rats only a few moonrises ago. She liked to play 'guess the poison' with him, a grotesque game of show and tell where if he got the disease right he would be allowed to leave. The man had been hallucinating, foaming at the mouth, desperately thirsty but too terrified of water to drink. He hadn't been able to tell his mother what it was, he'd never heard of rabies before. This meant he had to stay with her, until the poor man finally died, his eyes rolled back into his head and his mouth locked open in a crusty circle.

"Can you check this packet of herbs for me?" Alcyone said, making him jump. "I don't want to take the wrong thing."

"Sure," he said, staring at it. "Yes, this is right; this is what we're looking for."

"Good," she said, swallowing down a handful with a grimace.

His memory of the poisoned man wouldn't leave him. He'd been so emaciated you could see the shape of his bones underneath his skin. In his madness, he'd slashed open his veins with his nails, wiping the blood on the wall in long vertical splashes. Rabies. *It's an animal disease.* That's what Eris had told him. *From dogs and wolves.*

Dogs and wolves.

A skin of cool calm layered itself over him like a healing blanket, bringing with it a wonderful lightness, a lightness of knowledge that he took hold of and hid in the depths of his mind like buried treasure so Nemesis wouldn't find it there. He reached back to the shelf and took hold of the small bottle of rabies that he'd nearly crushed under his foot.

"Alcyone, I've found a poison." he said, reaching for her hand. "It's called rabies. I watched my mother test it on a prisoner. It's made from an animal disease. It can kill large mammals; dogs and wolves. We can take it and use it to infect Nemesis and her army."

"Rabies?" she said, shaking her head. "But what about the prisoner? The one she tested this rabies on, what happened to him?"

"He went mad… he died."

"Then what use is it? It won't just kill the wolves; it will kill us too."

"She gave me a drop of something, a protection medicine, that stops your body getting the disease. She always makes them. She doesn't want to risk infecting herself. That means I'll be okay. It won't make me ill."

"But what about the rest of us?"

"You need to gather up as many people as you can and get back to the White Plains. Guard the portal.

Keep away until it's done."

"You mean you want to do this on your own?"

"Take the medicines we've gathered back to safety. Go home and get well and I'll fix this mess; my mess."

"Maybe I don't want to be sent home like a child!" she said, fire flashing through her eyes. "Wouldn't it be better for both of us to go back to the White Plains, to make a plan and to think this through? We can talk to Nocturne and my other generals and put together a team. You can't infect them on your own, they'll kill you."

"I can't come with you. I can't come through the portal."

"Why not?"

"I'm infected too, infected with something else; with my connection with these wolves, by the fact that my blood created them."

"That's ridiculous! Infected? Those wolves are nothing to do with you. Nemesis forced you; she *stole* your blood. Come on, if you help me we can go now; we can get to the portal before the turn of the hand moves towards dusk…"

"You know I can hear them, Alcyone." He grabbed her arms, pulling off his mask and turning her towards him so she had to look him in the eyes. "I told you I could hear them in my head and it's all the time now. They talk to me because I am one of them, I'm one of the pack. Because I created them with my blood. And Nemesis. I can hear Nemesis too. And, well, I think they can hear me."

A shadow flickered across her face, her brow creasing.

"They… they've been *listening* to us?"

"No. I can shut them out, but it's hard to keep focused. They are on the edges of my mind all the time, pushing… prodding… and the training you tried to give me, the way to get through the portal… it's like opening a gate; it lets them in, it lets *Nemesis* in. I can't go with you. I can't risk them knowing about you and everyone else you've protected. That means I'm stuck here, and if I am then I might as well try to do some good."

She shook her head. "Why didn't you tell me this before!"

"I was scared that you would leave me, I'd just found you and… I didn't want to lose you."

"Oh, Strife!" she pressed her head into his chest, hugging him tightly.

As he rested his cheek on her hair his confidence faded.

Could he do this? Could he let her go?

"I've got a plan," he said. "It's risky but I think I can do it. Nemesis is desperate, she is calling to me because she wants me to help her."

"Great. Good idea. Help Nemesis and those wolves to kill more people. That's going to fix all of this." She shivered, pulling away from him and wrapping her arms around her chest.

"I can be their alpha. If I work with Nemesis and join in her war, I can use the wolves to weaken Eris' defences, then when the moment is right," he said holding up the small bottle. "I will use this to finish all of them. Nemesis will be dead; the wolves will be gone and Eris will be on her knees. Then... *then* we deploy your army, finish my mother for good, and reclaim this city for ourselves."

"It's too dangerous," she said. "If Nemesis can see inside your head, maybe she will see these plans too."

"No, she won't. I've spent my whole life hiding memories. It's one thing I know I'm good at," he said. "But this does have to look real. I must be alongside her every moment of the day, to fight with her, to be her general. She should believe that I'm hers, that I'm part of the pack. And the wolves must believe it too. So, I must make myself believe it... just for a little while. Then they won't suspect me and giving them the poison will be easy."

Those eyes, her beautiful eyes, scrutinising him, swallowing him away, digging inside him, seeing him, seeing everything.

"I can't come with you to the White Plains until all the wolves are dead, Alcyone. There isn't a choice."

"If I agree to this then there's one condition. I need to see you. Just like I did with Zephyrus. We will meet somewhere safe. I need to know that you are still... you."

"But that's dangerous too."

"It's not negotiable."

"Okay then... if that's what it takes to keep you away from here, it's a deal."

A smile smudged her lips and was gone, sucked away by a shudder of fever. Sitting her down on the floor, he hugged her shivering body close to him and she rested her head on his shoulder, the weight of it feeling decent; right. He made a vow to remember the sea salt and pine cone smell of her hair, the tickle of her breath on his neck and the weight of her, the goodness of her… to let it be his shield to protect him against the days ahead, against what he would have to do and become. As the medicine started its work inside her, he closed his eyes too, knowing this might be his last sleep free of nightmares.

With their masks tight against their faces, they fired up the incinerator at the back of the university. His mother used it to get rid of the evidence, to obliterate whatever scraps of flesh and broken bones were left after her experiments. They took it in turns to throw each of the bottles of poison into its white cleansing heat, and despite the warmth, he shivered, crossing his arms as the flames danced and destroyed.

"Is that all of them?" she asked.

The melted pile of glass sizzled and hissed.

"All but one," he said.

The weight of the small bottle of rabies inside his tunic felt heavier than it should.

"Now I think it's time for you to go home," he said.

She nodded at him, saying nothing.

Her fever had broken but so had her strength. He

had to help her to walk. Clinging to him, she kept apologising for her weakness, but he didn't mind; the slower they moved, the more turns of the hand they would have together. They journeyed out of the back of the university, heading towards the small scrubby forest, sitting forgotten in the shadows of its tallest tower—the Gold Tower.

"It's just here, inside the trees. It's funny that so many coins are spent on castles and fortresses but the best places to keep secrets are the ones nobody notices."

They held onto each other and he closed his eyes, his throat tight.

"I have to leave you here, I can't watch you go through the portal," he said. "I can't risk it being in my memory."

"Are you sure you can't come with me? The White Plains are hundreds of pacometers away; perhaps the distance will remove your connection to them?"

"Even if it did, what would we do then? If Nemesis wins, her wolves will kill us all and if Eris wins, well, the humiliation of this… she'll never let her citizens forget. It's the best plan we have. And you will have work to do too; you need to get your soldiers ready to strike. Once both sides have exhausted their fiercest warriors, once they are on their knees, then you have the most important part, more important than mine—you must come and end it, you must come and bring peace."

"You promise to meet me in ten sunsets? Here at dawn?"

"But I will be changed… I must play a part, to live

and be someone else. I'm not sure I want you to see me like that."

"I don't care."

"Do you always get your way?" he asked.

"Yes," she said. "Yes, I do!"

His smile took him by surprise, effervescing inside him. He couldn't remember the last time he'd felt such happiness so he let it go and she caught it too. Holding onto each other, they laughed with wonderful stomach-cramping joy, setting it free like birdsong echoing around the trees. Whatever happened, however all this ended, he'd never forget his time with her and this pleasure that she had given him. She and Zephyrus were gifts he didn't deserve. They were of Gaea's line, yet it didn't matter, none of that mattered; they had given him a purpose, they would bring the world hope and they meant his life was finally worth something.

As they pulled apart, the forest moved around them and they both lifted their daggers as a straggle of bodies appeared from the trees. He smiled as one of them raced towards him, swallowing him into a hug.

"You made it," he said, holding the boy away from him.

Doros looked like a street dog, his teeth were yellow and his skin was filthy, like he'd been sprayed with silt. He blasted Strife with a fierce grin, his brown eyes shining.

"Not all of us made it," he said. "The wolves took the weakest, the ones that couldn't run."

A huddle of prisoners shuffled forward, half-starved. Some of them were already trembling with withdrawal from the light vials, but they were here, they were alive.

"What about Helene and Arion?" Alcyone asked.

"We split up, I don't know what happened to them," Doros said. "We took refuge in the museum, it kept us safe, sealed off its doors from the wolves. We found some of the city dwellers there too. We said we would go back for them, once we knew it was safe."

"I swear that museum has the soul of Gaea herself inside it," Alcyone said. "It saved me too."

Strife nodded, his shame etched deep. Once they defeated Eris, the museum would be the first place he would go, on his knees, begging for forgiveness.

"Don't worry, we will keep a twenty-four turn of the hand watch," Alcyone said. "If any of them make it here we'll look after them."

"Doros," Strife said. "Would you mind helping Alcyone? She is recovering from an infection and will need a strong shoulder like yours to support her while she teaches you how to use the portal."

"Of course," Doros said, his face flushing with pride.

Strife rested his head against hers, pressing their skin together, the two pendants around her neck brushing against his throat.

"Ten sunsets, don't forget," she whispered.

"I won't. Safe journey, all of you," he said, stepping back and nodding to Doros to help keep her upright.

"You aren't coming with us?" Doros asked,

frowning at him.

"Not yet," he said, "but soon."

Alcyone's eyes were fat with tears and she took hold of both his hands. He squeezed her fingers and pulled away again, because he knew that if he waited just another minute he wouldn't be able to let her go.

He walked to the edge of the forest, the base of the Gold Tower glimmering in the sunshine. After counting to one hundred, he turned around. Part of him hoped she would be there, following behind him, but the forest lay quiet and still.

Sickness whirled like a cyclone in his stomach and he had to reach for one of the trees to keep his balance. Something grazed his neck, something hanging down from his backpack. The pendant. Zephyrus' pendant; she'd left it for him. Smiling, he hooked it over his head, holding it in his hand, feeling the comfort of its warmth before tucking it deep inside his tunic.

No more stalling, it was time.

This is for all of us, for our future and for all those who have gone before.

And her; this is for her.

Opening his arms, he pushed his chest up to the sky and roared. The noise bellowed around the trees and the darkest part of him woke from its box of shadows, setting free all that he'd worked so hard to forget and contain, all the terrible things that he'd seen and done and defeated so many moonrises ago in the training grounds, with Zephyrus by his side. The dark thing smiled as it gorged on the torture, the killing, the mutilation of flesh, bones, and minds that his mother had made him bear witness to. And as it grew fresh and fat, he refilled the empty box with light. In went Alcyone and Zephyrus, in went his morality, his love and all that made him good; all of it he crushed inside. And after he made this hideous exchange, he let go of the blockade to the pack and he let the wolves enter his head with their violence, their hunger and their call for blood. Staggering under the weight of them, he opened his mind just a little bit wider, to make one final connection.

"*STRIFE? STRIFE*"

"*Nemesis? Where are you?*"

"*The training grounds. Come to me, come.*"

A fat pigeon hopped above him in the branches, irritating him with its stupid noise. Pulling a knife, he let it fly and it hit its target with a thud, the bird falling dead at his feet, the blade sticking through its heart. Staring at it, he felt nothing as he watched a trail of blood leak from its beak. He yanked the dagger out, wiped it on his leg and kicked the bird's limp body into the trees.

I'm coming to you Nemesis. I'm coming.

Chapter Fourteen
The White Soldiers

THEIR MAKESHIFT HOSPITAL STILL overflowed with patients but the groans and cries had been replaced by a hubbub of chatter. Sitting up in their beds, their wounds healing and their light-vial addictions sweated into knotted blankets, the prisoners from the Pitch were revealing black-toothed smiles.

As Alcyone glanced around the ward, it filled her with a warm glow of hope. Many more people than she'd anticipated had made it through the portal and their small community had doubled in size. Their new citizens were blessed with much-needed skills—farmers, carpenters, tanners, and builders. Plans were being made to turn their tented shelters into wooden cottages which would grow the small clearing into a busy village. They were going to double the size of their plantation, using the seeds from the healing herbs she had brought with her to cultivate medicines.

A zigzag of leather hammocks was strung through the hospital's patched tents and the inside bustled with activity. A fluster of young people hurried behind one of the healers who was teaching them about fever-reducing herbs. Remembering her own recent sickness, Alcyone clasped the bandage on her forearm. The wolf bite had been closed with haphazard stitching from a red-faced apologetic trainee and it would leave her with a scar. Not that she minded; she believed that scars were like memories and if you kept their origins close to your heart they taught you lessons—scars were the marks of war.

Two of the refugees, a young boy from the Pitch and the first girl they'd found in the Flowlands apartments were playing sword fights with sticks. The boy had lost his left hand to the wolves, but he showed great agility with his right, blocking the moves of his challenger, his wrinkled nose a squash of concentration. Alcyone smiled at their determined faces and skinny legs, remembering how she too used to play the same game with Zephyrus.

A tap on her shoulder made her leap into the air and yank two daggers from her belt.

"By Hades, Alcyone. It's me, it's Nocturne."

Nocturne raised his hands and the children stopped their play fighting to stare at them, their mouths opening into two shiny circles.

Embarrassed, she lowered the knives back to her side.

"I'm sorry, Nocturne. I'm a little jumpy these days."

"You have nothing to fear here, Alcyone."

"We shouldn't take the safety of this camp for granted," she said. "The battles we think of as far away could reach our door too."

"We share responsibility for the protection of this camp, remember. It is not your burden to shoulder alone. Now, how are things here?"

"Good. There are no new casualties today and those that are still here seem to be recovering. Strife was right about the prisoners from the Pitch, they have more fight in them than all of us put together."

Nocturne nodded, grinning at the children who had resumed their mock battle.

"I can see that."

"I wish my father were here to see this, he would be proud of us, he would be so excited about the medicines too."

"I'm sure Asclepius would be beaming with approval of what you are doing here. Zephyrus always told me that he was more comfortable healing people than he was fighting, and that your mother was the real warrior, not him."

"I can hardly remember what they look like... and Zephyrus' face is fading too."

"That doesn't matter, they are etched in your heart, in your courage, in your actions. And Poseidon himself has given you his blessing. Their strength is with you, always."

"I hope so, Nocturne. I fear I will need it. Are the generals ready to meet?"

"We are."

The clack of the children's sticks stayed in her head as she followed Nocturne to the centre of their community. Nine sunsets had passed since she'd said goodbye to Strife, and her memories of him, unlike those of her parents, of his kindness, his determination and his fear were fixed in her memory. Where was he now? What if he was lying injured, like he had been on the roof of the museum, surrounded by a growing pool of blood? Brushing these morbid thoughts from her mind, she reached for her amber pendant, reminding herself that its twin glowed against Strife's heart too. If anything went wrong she would know.

Walking next to their training grounds, they passed a group firing arrows at straw-filled scarecrows while others fought hand-to-hand. She spotted Helene and Doros from the Pitch sparring; they were both shaping up to be fine sergeants. Still, compared to the army of wolves and Red Guards, their troops were paltry and the majority of her soldiers were still so young. The violence of the battle taking place in the city made her realise how naïve they had been. Strife's wolves were clearing the way and she knew that they wouldn't have stood a chance against Eris without them.

A smell of fresh pine wood seeped from the open doorway of their new meeting hut. Stamping the snow from her boots for longer than she needed to, she prepared herself for the meeting, taking in a long breath and summoning a surge of strength from Poseidon's gift as she stepped inside.

Pandia, the youngest of her generals at only thirteen, leaned over a leather map of Eristonia. Tiny, like a faerie, she whipped around the table, scratching on marks with a charcoal stick, her long, fine hair the colour of summer fog. Acting as their nocturnal scout, she had spent the last nine nights in the city, following the movement of battle lines. Quick and soundless, she was an excellent tracker, a fearless climber, and a bullseye shot with the crossbow that never left her side. Her final general, Helios stood still and calm, leaning on his sword, following Pandia's every move. Sixteen, with beautiful golden curls and azure blue eyes, Helios was as handsome as a first-God, and shined brightly with natural optimism. When he saw her, he smiled and it was like a blast of pure sunshine, warming the gnarls of coldness in her heart.

Nocturne pressed his fist to his forehead as she walked past him to the head of the table.

"I wish you wouldn't do that," she said, redness stinging her cheeks.

"It is a mark of the highest respect, Alcyone, that's all," Nocturne said.

"Then wait until I've done something to earn it."

He grinned at her, shaking his head. "You are too hard on yourself."

"Maybe so, but our hardships haven't even started yet. Once this battle is won, once we have got through the war ahead, then I might accept your show of respect. For now, we have much to catch up on. Pandia, will you go first?"

"The destruction of the city continues at speed, Alcyone," Pandia said, her voice like a rustle of leaves in the wind. "The wolves and the Red Guards are well matched and the battle for the Flowlands begins each nightfall. Eris has freed the vryloakas from the forests and pulled in the armies of some of her loyal families, most of them from the Valley of Shadows, east of the mountains. The bloodline of Hecate is at her side but Moros' clan is missing, as is Morpheus'. It is good for us that they are staying away. Once Strife joins us, once we show that our dynasties can stand together, we can ask them to fight with us."

Strife had told her of the suitors coming to woo his mother and of Eris embarrassing Morpheus and turning Moros away. Could they be persuaded to help them or were they watching too, plotting to make a strike of their own?

"Are the vryloakas fighting?" she said, remembering the call of them in the forest and their hypnotising promises, the thought of it all bringing a whirl of sickness to her stomach.

"They are more of a distraction as their voices seem to muddle the pack. They are having a wonderful time flapping around, growing fat on wolf blood. They've not been so well fed for many centuries," Pandia said, her top lip wrinkling.

"And our portal?"

"It is safe… as far as I know. I am keeping it under constant guard. We are struggling to get some of the refugees through as many are too sick to make the shift, so we've set up a holding station inside the university under the Gold Tower. It's a little risky, but there isn't anything stored there that would be of interest to scavengers and the battle is so intense, I don't think Eris or Nemesis care much for the world outside their frontline."

"What of the castle?" Alcyone asked. "You have been watching it, Helios. It hasn't been taken?"

"No, Eris has it well protected," Helios said. "She has a perfect view of the city from her Pinnacle Room at the top and she sends out her crows as scouts. Though the wolves treat them like snacks if they fly too low. I must say it's the one highlight of this war, seeing those hideous birds disappear down a hellhound's throat. There is a kind of justice from Hades in that somewhere."

"I watched a large cluster of crows disappear out last night," Pandia said. "They were flying away from the city, which means Eris is scouting further afield. Maybe she's looking for more allegiances or a place to escape to in case the castle does fall?"

"How long do we wait this out, Alcyone?" Nocturne said, stepping forward. "While we sit here watching more civilians die. Some of them are trapped in the Flowlands, barricaded into their homes with no way out until this fighting is done or they starve, whichever comes first."

"The end is in sight, Nocturne," said Helios. "If Eris is using the vryloakas then she must be getting desperate. Nemesis and Strife are also taking huge losses. We know that the wolves are able to re-spawn, but this seems to be slowing down and they have a different problem to deal with."

"What is that?" Alcyone asked.

"Food," Nocturne said, and Helios nodded his agreement. "Their hunger is insatiable. They have ripped through the livestock supplies as well as most of their prisoners. It means their numbers are falling as those who die of their hunger are not being replaced by new ones."

"And Strife?" Alcyone asked. "Have you seen him?"

"He never leaves Nemesis' side, he is at the front of every battle; the wolves follow all his commands, it's like some kind of black magic," Pandia said. "He seems… very close to them all."

"That is the whole point," Alcyone said. "It's only been nine sunsets and he has made great inroads, gaining Nemesis' absolute trust and weakening both sides. It won't be long until he can finish them with the rabies poison, then as Eris celebrates and licks her wounds we will be ready to take her and her castle and put an end to all of this for good."

As she looked around the room a shadow passed over Pandia's face. Night after night she went out to the battlefields, keeping notes on tactics, fighting styles and the number of deaths, reporting all this horror back to Alcyone without question. This burden would take its toll on the hardiest of warriors. Even Helios looked weary. He'd been watching the portals and the castle, sweeping up civilians, saving them from the carnage that Strife had unleashed with her blessing.

"I have put too much on you," she said, lowering her eyes. "I should be out there with you, I should be risking my own neck in the battlegrounds, not sitting here like a fat queen bee waiting to be fed scraps of information."

"You and Nocturne are our best fighters, it is right you are here to train the new soldiers," Helios said, resting his hand on her shoulder. "This is a good plan… the best plan we have. You have put your trust in Strife, as Zephyrus did before you. We are with you, Alcyone."

"We are with you," they all said, raising their fists to their foreheads.

The sign of her royal bloodline, there again, even though she'd told them countless times to stop doing it. Opening her mouth to protest, she closed it again when she saw the sadness in their faces. They needed this; they needed the old customs to boost their courage and keep them going, and if she kept denying her dynasty she would only be disrespecting the most loyal advisors she had.

"We won't have to wait much longer. I go into the city to see Strife in one sunset," Alcyone said. "Then we will know the final plan."

"We only ask you one thing. For you to make one promise to us," Pandia said. "If Strife shows any sign of… disloyalty, then he must be treated as our enemy and dealt with in the same way."

"I know that," Alcyone said, her hand moving to her pendant. "But I won't need to. Strife is with us."

"I hope so, I truly do," Pandia said.

"Right then," Helios said.

He bustled around the map, easing away the tension. "Let's go over our own strategy again so you can make sure Strife is clear when you see him, Alcyone. Once the wolves fall, Strife will pretend to surrender to his mother and this is how we will enter the castle…"

She had listened to this plan over and over and it all seemed so easy; too easy. What had they forgotten? What of the other clans? Whose side would they be on once the war in the city reached its bloody finale? Pandia drew out the lines again for the hundredth time, their soldiers marked as white pins. But what were they really? A ragtag of children and prisoners, trained using substandard, filched weapons for less than half a cycle of the Moon. Were they mad, stupid, or both? Lowering her head, she closed her eyes, gripping the edge of the table, her nails digging into the wood.

"All will be well, Alcyone," Nocturne said, resting his hand on her shoulder. "We will fight, we will protect our own, and we will live or die in honour just like our forefathers. There is nothing for us to lose here."

"I know, Nocturne, but I made this plan. I am responsible, not just for our soldiers but for our civilians too, for all our lives."

"We are responsible for one another, the weight of this rests on all our shoulders. That is how it works here, you should know that by now."

Pandia shifted the marks on the map again and Helios leaned in towards her, moving her pins wider apart with a grin, ducking from the swat of her hand as she put them back again.

"I could not have done any of this without you all,"

she said, taking hold of his arm. "Thank you."

"You would do very well without us, Alcyone," Nocturne said. "But we are glad to help you. We are grateful for all that you've given us. For this new community, for this freedom."

"Let's hope it lasts," she said. "For if we fail who will take up our banner? Who will protect these people?"

"Kratos could be out there somewhere," he said. "Once Eris is gone he might come back, he might help us. The map that got you here, the chimes that you heard what if they *were* his…"

"If they were his, and if he did give me the map of the portals, then he should be ashamed. Ashamed of not helping his son."

"Who knows what happened all those years ago, what Eris did to him, where she sent him? He might not even be in this world, he could be stuck somewhere in between. And he *has* helped his son, if he brought you here, if he gave you and Zephyrus that map and this place of refuge then he has given his son something to fight for, given him friendship and trust."

"Maybe so," Alcyone said with a grunt. "But it might be too little too late."

"All will be well," he said. "You will see Strife on the morrow and he will settle your doubts, remind us of our purpose and how close we are to victory."

"Let's hope so, Nocturne. No matter how many times we go over our plan to take the castle, none of it matters unless he succeeds. The safety of all of our community and of all our futures rests on Strife."

Chapter Fifteen

Battle Lines

THE THWACK AND SLICE of Strife's sword had become his jarring symphony. Riding the largest of the wolves, a silver beast with a streak of black across its nose, he could feel its strength coursing through him, speeding them forward as one. His diamond sword had been waiting for him in the armoury and it stayed with him always now, sharp and light, his brother in war. He could see with a thousand eyes, hear with a thousand ears, smell, taste and live a thousand lives. Conducting this orchestra every day with the pack by his side and his blade in his hand, he felt invincible.

A bright full Moon lit their way as they galloped inside the city walls. Night after night of fighting had pushed their battle lines backwards and forwards, but tonight they had taken the advantage and were closing in on the castle.

The blue bricks of the Flowlands were stinging his

eyes after the muddy brown vista of their camp, and they looked alien to him, a place where he had lived a different life.

Sharp teeth snapped at his ears and he swiped at his head. The vryloakas were an irritant, feeding off his soldiers, muddling the pack's communication with their sickening whispers. The thing flapped around him again, grappling at his hair with its clawed toes. Thrusting his fist into the air, he closed his fingers around its neck and squeezed. Its teeth bulged, snapping, still trying to find flesh to bite. He slammed it against his thigh until its back snapped, feeding its remains to his wolf.

Riding a beast as black as the Pitch, Nemesis galloped up next to him, her face splashed with blood and her dreadlocks flying behind her like Medusa's snakes.

"They are falling back," she said. "Push forward, PUSH FORWARD!"

Echoing her words in his head, he spread this command out to his brothers and sisters. The wolves howled, hearing his word, lifting their heads to rip into the Red Guards. Fast learners, they were adept at avoiding the swirl of the fire-fuelled swords and they ducked and leapt in a beautiful choreography of killing. Riding off along the left flank, Nemesis spiked a guard through the chest with her long, metal spear.

Racing up and down the frontline, he slashed and gouged, clearing the way of vryloakas, keeping his army safe, helping them regroup, seeing and feeling all their thoughts and the strength of their bodies.

Forward, forward, keep moving. Attack! Attack!

A Red Guard slashed at the nose of his wolf and he pulled on the scruff of its neck, yanking it to the side, clenching the muscles in his thighs, his makeshift leather saddle sliding away from him. The guard moved quickly, ripping open three wolves, its fire-sword spinning, splashing blood across the road. Slicing forward again, it cut through the back of his wolf's thighs and it fell, smashing to the floor, trapping his legs under its heavy chest.

To me. Now.

Three wolves left their formation, leaping on the soldier, ripping out his neck and chewing down hunks of flesh.

Fight now, feed later.

Stopping, they eyed him for a moment before throwing the guard's body to one side and helping to free him from the dead wolf. Jumping up, he raced to join the throng of fighters, attacking on foot, his sword twirling fast and strong.

We rest at dawn. We feed at dawn.

Opening his mind wider and wider, he could feel every cut; every death; every victory.

The army of wolves was *his*, all of them, all of them…

Then he saw Eris circling above his head, riding a fat dragon, her hair matted and her white clothes, always so pristine, spotted with black. There had been no sign of her for many moonrises as she'd locked herself in her castle, too important to get her hands dirty. As she swooped lower and he scanned the battlefield, he realised that she had come out to survey her losses because his wolves were winning. They were outnumbering her soldiers three to one.

The smell of defeat; that's what had pulled her out of her sanctuary.

An arrow speared the wolf next to him through the eye and it slumped to the ground.

Keep close, stay close to me.

Swift as the wind, another took its place by his side.

"I can see you, Strife."

Her voice jarred. He had grown used to the ebb and flow of the pack inside his mind. They had no need for words, and Nemesis was the only person he'd heard speak for nine sunsets.

Another arrow flew towards his face and one of his wolves jumped into its path, catching it in his jaws.

His mother swooped lower.

"I see you've trained your new pets well," she said.

"They are not pets, they are soldiers. Are you too cowardly to fight with your own troops, mother?"

"Too wise, my child."

"I am not a child."

"So, I see. You fight well. If you were on my side I could almost be proud."

"I care nothing for your opinion," he said, slicing off an arm and then rounding through a neck, keeping his rhythm. Realising then with a flush of shame that he was showing off and that he still wanted to impress her, that he still craved her approval, even now after everything she'd done to him.

"You are of royal blood, but these hell's wolves, they are base. Is that how you want your history written? Alongside these animals? Why don't you join me? If you prove your loyalty I will name you as my heir."

Dropping his sword to his side, he stared up at her wide-eyed, bodies falling around him.

"What did you say?"

"You heard me, Strife. You will be my heir."

Heir to Eris. Words he never thought he'd ever hear uttered, not from his mother's lips. A sludge of confusion blurred the clarity that he'd felt all those Moons ago when he'd made his plan, when he'd taken his chances with Nemesis, when he'd let Alcyone go.

He pushed her name away, not wanting the pack to hear it.

A horrible pain like a needle through his eyes made him stumble and the wolves closed in to protect him.

Who was he? What was he?

"Think on it, Strife. The offer won't stand for long," Eris said.

He straightened up, lifting his sword. "The fight isn't over yet, mother, and you're losing."

"Don't be so naïve, Strife. I never lose."

The dragon flew higher and she headed off back towards the castle, lifting her bow and arrow and calling to the remainder of her soldiers.

Turning to the battle, he saw new colours in between the red armour of her guards. Suits of blue, of green, and of yellow, and a new muddle of weapons clashing with his wolves' jaws. Many of these soldiers were untrained and they fell fast. A young boy raced towards him, his weapon raised, his mouth open, not in the cry of a warrior but in terror. Hesitating, he held his sword still and one of his wolves had to jump in to protect him, pinning the attacker to the ground.

A boy.

His mother's rallying cry made the back of his neck prickle.

Was he going to let his wolves murder child soldiers?

Eris. Nemesis. Alcyone.

Who were his family? Who was he?

You are our maker and our king.

The pack knew, they were clear and strong and never faltered.

They were all that mattered. He was the alpha, the leader of this rampage of wolves and commander of a great army who were on track to win the greatest city on Earth.

"Retreat!" His call trumpeted through the ranks. "Retreat!"

A cacophony of howls echoed through the streets as he raised his sword to the sky.

Those near to the buildings, sleep here, protect and guard.

All others, go back beyond the wall, back to our camp. Retreat! Retreat!

Eat; sate your hunger.

Brown fur streamed past him, dragging bodies with them out beyond the Flowland gates. As the wolves pulled back, the civilian soldiers let their swords rest to their sides.

Tomorrow night. Tomorrow night the castle would be his.

"What are you doing? We almost had them!" Riding out in front of him, Nemesis' face was thunderous. "We have another half a turn of the hand before the Sun rises, why are you calling to retreat?"

"She is sending in untrained soldiers; boys."

"Then she is desperate and this means it is our time to strike."

"Our battle is not with children. The night's fighting is over, Nemesis. Tomorrow we will take the castle."

Staring at him, the spear in her hand twitched. Keeping his chin high, he held her gaze, his face stony. Whatever her thoughts, he would always win because he had the alpha position and she didn't.

"Okay, Strife," she said. "We do this your way. We will finish it on the next sunset."

Nodding, he turned to face the remaining straggle of soldiers. "Go back to your families, gather your belongings, and run. Tonight, we will give you one chance to escape, to get away from the city. Eris doesn't care for you; she is using you. We will be back tomorrow night and if you are here too, we will kill you."

A handful of them dropped their swords and ran

while the others looked from him back up to the castle, stuck to the spot, so downtrodden and terrorised they had no idea what to do next.

Sighing, he turned back to Nemesis. "Shall we go?"

"Come up here with me and we can ride back to camp together."

Slotting his sword into the sheath across his back, he took hold of her outstretched hand and jumped up behind her. Wrapping his arms around her waist, he closed his eyes, the smell of a thousand deaths rising from the leather of her tunic.

"You should send some wolves to keep guard of the buildings to the west of the museum too," Nemesis said as they rode past it. "We have made good ground and we don't want to lose it.

The museum. He'd forgotten all about the museum.

It looked older; tired, charred, and blackened on one side by the fire he'd caused. His throat tightened. What would happen if he went inside? Would it still try to kill him?

"Think not on the past," Nemesis said, following his gaze. "None of that matters. We are wolves now."

The roll of the wolf's paws soothed him as they raced past the bloodied bodies littering the streets, galloping out through the city gates. They had made their camp in the old training grounds and its tall fences and position on higher ground gave them clear views of the city. It also meant the armoury's supplies were protected from use by Eris' soldiers. On his first night, he'd gone inside to get his father's old sword from its shrine on the wall, wanting to protect it from marauders. But, when he bashed at the case it bounced back at him, unyielding, protected by reinforced glass. Using the back of a hammer, he clawed at the rusty bolts but they too refused to let go, leaving him to smash at the wood until it finally fell to the floor and split in two. As he reached inside to grab the handle a cold breeze twisted around his arm, pinching his skin. Shivering, he stepped back, the wind rising and wrapping around his chest, squeezing him in a blustery embrace before melting away.

"Hell's Gates, what was that?" his voice echoed in the silence and the wolves outside howled. He stood with his father's beautiful sword raised high, waiting for something else to happen, but the room was still and quiet. Once he had the sword, he didn't know what to do with it, so he dug a hole near his hammock and hid it there under earth and leaves. When he dropped it into the ground it felt like he was burying his father too, and the strength of his grief sent the wolves into a flurry of confusion. Why was he sad? Their alpha had no father because *they* were his family, *they* were all that counted…

His thoughts drifted back to the boy from the battle, the terror on his face, his arms straining under the weight of his sword and his armour hanging off him like a dressing-up costume. How old had he been? Eleven? Twelve? There weren't that many cycles of the Moon between them, but he felt a hundred times older;

a thousand. That boy would never reach manhood, because of Eris.

No, because of me.

"You are still thinking like a half-God," Nemesis said. "You have to stop it, you are upsetting the pack."

The gates of the training grounds opened for them and the guards on the gates howled as they passed by. The wolves liked to sleep in burrowed holes and the camp resembled an enormous muddy field. Nemesis had a base at the centre in an old guard's hut but Strife preferred to stay in a hammock, rigged up high in the trees of the training ground where he and Nocturne had battled a dragon what felt like a thousand moonrises ago. The wolf bowed his head at Strife as he dismounted before sloping off towards its underground bed.

"Come, Strife. Talk with me," Nemesis said, putting her arm over his shoulder.

Too tired to protest, he let her lead him into the hut. She lit a small fire as he removed the backpack of staves that he kept for the vryloakas. Stabbing his sword into the earth, he watched the reflection of the flames licking at the blade. His eyes were growing heavy from the heat, but he knew he wouldn't be able to sleep.

"You cannot let yourself be troubled by them," she said.

"By who?"

"By the tribe that is no longer your own. The half-Gods and humans. They are not destined to share this world with us for much longer. Surely it is better for them to die in battle as warriors than trembling in their beds or as prisoners in our cages?"

"They were children, Nemesis. They should be at home with their mothers, not fighting the wars of their elders. I didn't expect it."

"Eris probably knew that. I fear those untrained soldiers were all for you."

"Why would they be for me?"

Kneeling in front of him, she took hold of both this hands in hers. "Your heart. It is your heart that weakens you. You still care for those that are not your clan. You still deny us, you even sleep as far away from us as you can, way up in the trees. Your mother knows this. She will use it against you."

"I am a wolf. I came here to you, remember. You needed me, you called me and I came. I am a wolf."

"You are *almost* a wolf."

The familiar stabbing pain came again and he cried out, clutching his head in his hands as it spread through him, breaking him apart like cracking ice. He screamed for it to kill him, to stop his heart and finish him just to make it go away. Then, like a rush of dust in the wind, it was gone.

Opening his eyes, he saw Nemesis leaning over him and felt the damp ground against his back. His muscles didn't want to follow his commands and he let her help him up onto a chair. She passed him a cup of water, but he had no grip and she grasped her hands around his to help him sip it. Focusing on her face, he tried to smile, swallowing hard so he didn't throw the water back up again.

"The pack and their connection to you, it comes from your bloodletting, of your royal creed," she said. "They have accepted you as their alpha and we would not have got this army organised without you. But you are still a half-God. Your mind is not used to the many others flowing into it; it is not adapting fast enough. The pain you have, it is because you are not yet one of us. Because you are *almost* a wolf. And these episodes will only get worse."

The pool of concern in her almond eyes pulled at his heart. Nemesis. His true family, his protector, his ally and his friend. At first, the pack had filled him with irritation, the constant calling, the howling and grunts, their need for command and the fact they had to have him with them always. But over the last few nights, sinking into the depth of their connection, he'd let go to them, to belonging, to being respected, to having authority. Had this always been his destiny? To run with Nemesis, to be a wolf and to bring an end to the era of half-Gods and humans?

As these thoughts swirled through him, he felt the vial of rabies digging into his skin, the poison wrapped up tightly in a rag wound around the top of his leg. Always there, waiting and judging him as it pressed into his flesh. Could he give the wolves up? Could he let them all go? What did Alcyone have to replace them? Child soldiers, not that different from those they had almost sent to their deaths today.

"You *must* take the final step," Nemesis said. "You must drink of their blood as they have of yours. I had to do this to connect to you and to stop the pain; this will free you from the bonds of half-Gods and humans forever. This will truly make you a wolf."

"Drink of their blood?"

She nodded, watchful, trying to listen to the worried flurry of his thoughts that he worked so hard to block from her. Could she hear them too? She knew he was hiding something from her. That much was certain.

"I will think on it," he said.

"Don't think for too long. It will kill you eventually, that pain. If you want to stay with us, if you really *are* a wolf, you have little choice."

"I am tired, I need to rest," he said.

"We have other things to think on too. The spawning has stopped, that means there are no new wolves. Our remaining wolves will need to make their own future and bring cubs into this world. We must protect some of them, keep them away from battle or we will be too few to survive." She paused. "If we don't establish them here we might need to use the whistle again, which would be dangerous for you."

The whistle. Gods. Would he ever be safe? Could she kill him again if she needed to? Probably. It was all about the pack. The pack. The pack.

"Do we have to talk about this now?"

"No, it can wait another moonrise. Let's win the castle and then we will speak again. Go now, child, get some sleep."

Coiling him in a hug of sticky leather, Nemesis whispered in his ear.

"You cannot trust Eris. She doesn't care for anyone but herself."

"I know that," he said. "Don't worry, Nemesis. I am yours. We will talk about the blood tomorrow, I promise."

She nodded, smiling at him and thumping him on the back.

"You are my family, Strife, through lineage and through wolf. We will be bound together for eternity and we will run free under our own command. It is the right decision. It is time for real change."

"Rest well," he said.

"See you on the morrow. See you for victory!"

Trudging to the trees on the edge of the training grounds, his body aching, his journey slow, the clouds skittered over the Sun, swallowing away the light in flickering bursts. Nine sunsets had passed since he'd said goodbye to Alcyone but it felt like nine lifetimes. Her face had faded in his mind, the clean smell of her replaced by the constant stench of death and wolf breath. Tomorrow at dawn he'd promised he would see her again. His hand automatically went to the pendant and it felt warm to his touch, as always. He'd seen the girl who moved like a shadow near their battlegrounds every night, and he knew she must be spying for Alcyone. To her watchful eye, his task must be progressing as planned. Both armies were thinning but his mother had taken the worst of the casualties, holed up in her palace; she had never been so weak. The time had arrived for him to use the rabies poison and to finish off the wolves so Alcyone could take the castle. But, but... the murmur of the pack burbled inside him like a rushing waterfall. They were his pack; *his* wolves and his old self had faded, so they were becoming everything to him as he was everything to them and he didn't know how much longer he could hide all his thoughts from them. How much longer he could protect her. It would be easier just to do as Nemesis asked, to drink their blood and go to them, to be with them forever.

"Am I wolf?" he whispered to himself as he climbed the tree to his hammock. "Or am I half-God?"

He lay with his eyes open, staring up at the leaves.

"Alcyone. Alcyone. Alcyone..." he whispered her name into the wind. "What am I? Who am I?"

Letting his tears go, they itched down his cheeks, and once they started he couldn't stop them. They were like endless rain, soaking his face and his ears, but they gave him no relief and no answers.

"By the Gods, I am lost," he said, choking on his own breath as he spoke to the sky.

"I am lost. I am lost. I am lost."

Chapter Sixteen
The Meeting

ALCYONE STRAPPED HER KNIFE belt around her waist and opened the door to her sleeping quarters, the cold air stinging her cheeks. Pandia followed closely behind, pulling her hood over her silver hair. The end of the night breathed in and out around them, shadows flicking free from their bounds, travelling wider than they should.

"Have you noticed that the darkness seems to be moving?" Alcyone said.

"The barriers between this world and the next are melting away," Pandia said, drawing her robe tighter across her chest. "Who knows what else the ground will vomit up if these wolves stay too long. The turn of the hand is not on our side, Alcyone."

Pressing her lips together, she stayed silent, irritated by Pandia's constant need to push her. They all knew that the time had come for them to make their move. Eris' troops were weak, the wolves were on the ascendant, and ten sunsets had passed. They were ready for the second stage of their plan; they were waiting for Strife to use the rabies poison to kill the pack.

As they headed out to the portal, fresh snow dusted the air and the first light of dawn pushed brightness into the shadows, shoving aside whatever creatures might be hiding there.

"You shouldn't meet him alone."

"I will be three pacometers from the portal, Pandia. I will be fine."

"They were strong last night. The wolves know how the Red Guards fight and are getting better at defeating them. Strife's confidence as their commander has also grown."

"That is the plan, he's following the plan."

"But he hasn't released the rabies virus."

"Then it isn't the right time."

"I have been watching him. He seems to be made for his role; he is good at leading them and the wolves love him in return. They rely on him, he is everything to them. It will be hard for him to leave them behind."

"What do you want me to say, Pandia?"

Alcyone clenched her fists, trying to stop her voice from rising.

"As far as I can see he is doing everything he said he would, but I cannot read his mind. I need to see him, to know if he has turned against us and if he has, then I will deal with it!"

"I still think I should come with you."

"No. I need to do this alone."

Nocturne suddenly appeared beside Pandia, and then Helios, hovering behind them.

"By Poseidon, why are *you* here? Don't any of you trust me?"

"We trust you, Alcyone, we are at your command, we are here to remind you that whatever happens today with Strife, you are not alone," Helios said. "But you cannot be swayed by your feelings for him. The wolves have slaughtered two thirds of Eris' soldiers, but the sheer volume of civilian casualties is unacceptable. It's time. The wolves must go."

"I *know* this! I don't need you all here reminding me of the plan that *I* made!"

Her shout echoed in the air, but their worry fuelled her own doubts. Why *hadn't* he released the virus? Why were the wolves still well? Why had he kept them strong for so long?

To weaken Eris, to get everything ready. To stick to the plan.

Their plan.

"Eris sent in untrained soldiers yesterday, young men and women, boys and girls. Strife saw them in battle and let his wolves attack them too," Pandia said.

"He is playing a part!" she said, looking around at all their frowning faces. "This has to look real, he is doing his job!"

"Okay, enough!" Nocturne said. "You also reported that he pulled back his troops soon after the new soldiers appeared, Pandia remember?"

Pandia glared at him and nodded.

"Let's stop this petty bickering. We are not here to fracture our pact, we are here to show you that we are stronger together. We are with you, Alcyone," Nocturne said.

"Yes, we are all with you, Alcyone," Helios said, turning to Pandia. "Aren't we?"

Pandia hesitated for a moment before closing her eyes and nodding.

"Of course, I am, of course I am with you."

Nocturne pressed his fist to Alcyone's heart, leaning down to rest his forehead against hers. *Stay strong*, his eyes said as they locked onto hers. *Stay strong.*

"Thank you; all of you," she whispered. "I will find you as soon as I return. Now you should go and sharpen up the weapons, we need to be ready to take that castle."

They smiled then, all three of them, and she smiled back. She hid her own fear, branding each of their faces into her mind just in case she needed to call on them later. They all hugged her before they trudged away and she stood alone in the snow, listening to the crunch of their retreating steps. Stamping the cold from her feet, she took in a slow breath, the rising Sun's warmth giving her strength. Closing her eyes, she tilted her face to the thin heat. There would soon be an end to war. Strife would make that happen and she trusted him to do it.

The portal shimmered in the half-light just like it had when she first tumbled through it with Zephyrus. The Sun had been shining then too, their new world so white and bright that she thought they had landed in heaven. Dusting snow off the triangle of stones she had laid so long ago to mark this place of travel, to mark their portal, she sent her brother a silent prayer before stepping into it. The transition that had once been painful now quick and smooth.

Rain dripped through the cluster of leaves and the clouds moved quickly in the woods of Eristonia. A swirl of wind filled her nose with the smell of fallen leaves and wet earth. Taking shelter under one of the largest trees, she waited, tucking in close to the trunk, the sweet smell of bark comforting her. She watched a rainbow curl across the sky, cutting across clouds that melted into the shape of seashells and fish. Since Poseidon had given her his protection, she missed the ocean always, like a dull ache. Moving out from under the trees, she raised her face to the sky, closing her eyes and letting the rain soak into her skin. If they got through this… *when* they got through this she would build her home by the sea and stay there forever…

"Alcyone?"

She turned towards his voice.

"*Strife?*"

Cuts and half-healed scars criss-crossed his cheeks, and his leather tunic, slick from the rain, had been slashed open from his shoulder to his hip, the tear patched together with fur. Blood, mud, and the Gods knew what else covered his face. His dark curls were filthy with knots and his lilac eyes were glazed, filled with something more than sadness, something… dark. Racing to hug him, she ignored the putrid smell that seeped from his clothes, only caring that he had come, that he was whole. He rested his head on her shoulder and the beat of his heart thrummed against hers, their arms winding around each other, fitting together in a perfect circle. But he only let her hold him for a few precious seconds before he pushed her away.

"I cannot stay here long, Alcyone. My connection is too strong now, I can only hide so much from my brothers and sisters."

Brothers and sisters?

"We have been watching you as we build our army," she said, trying to sound bright and positive. "I am so proud of all you have done and we have many, many refugees now in the White Plains. You were right about the prisoners, about the ones who came from the Pitch. They are some of our best fighters."

"How many. How many do you have? To fight?"

"Three hundred, maybe more."

"It is a paltry number."

"It… it will be enough once the wolves are gone."

His face crinkled and he put his hand to his forehead, staggering back towards one of the trees.

"Are you… are you okay?"

"The pack, their voices, the connection… I am not made like them, it… sometimes it hurts."

"This is a sign that it is time to stop. It is time to end these wolves and come back to me. We know the people that Eris is sending into battle are untrained children. It means she is weak and the wheel of fortune turns our way."

"Nemesis speaks many truths too, Alcyone. The strength that we have as a family, as a pack, it's like nothing I've ever known. I am one of them. I belong."

"They are animals! You are *not* like them."

"Aren't I? I lead them, kill with them, kill *for* them. This thing we have, that I created with my blood, it is… special. We protect each other, we don't even need to speak; it all falls into place like a melody."

"You have gone deep, Strife, as you promised, but it is time to pull back. These wolves, they use us for food, they cannot take over our world, they *cannot* be the future. You are not one of them, you are one of us!"

"Nemesis told me that if I drink their blood, I will be wolf. Full wolf."

"What are you *talking* about? You will never be a wolf!"

"You don't know anything, Alcyone. You don't know what I am, what I've become."

"Show me your pendant!"

Grabbing his tunic, she scratched around his neck for the chain, yanking on it so hard she pulled his face next to hers, their noses almost touching. The darkness in his eyes drifted away, letting a little of the old Strife out, scared and young and brimming with self-doubt.

"This is Zephyrus' pendant. Zephyrus, my brother and your best friend. Remember him?"

Water filled his eyes and she yanked at his neck again, glad of the reaction, scrabbling around for her own pendant. She let them connect so the amber stones sitting in the bottom of each vial glowed.

"I am your family, Strife. Not these… things, these wolves. It is time for them to go. It is time for Nemesis to go!"

"Nemesis has protected me since I was a child; she is my family too." He choked back a sob.

"I am in the abyss with them, Alcyone, and I don't know how to find my way back."

"She has groomed you for this, Strife. She cares only for herself, for destroying all that is left of the good in this world."

A spill of tears snaked down his cheeks and he grasped her hand, grasped it and raised it to his heart.

"You are so good, Alcyone."

"As are you!"

"I don't know if I am good or bad. I don't know who I am; *what* I am. I just know that the pain, the thunder of agony in my head, and the need of my brothers and sisters, it is too great now; it is everything. You must go, you must go and hide and we can never meet again. The White Plains, they can be a home for you. We will… we will stay away."

"No! This isn't you, this isn't who you are!"

"I have no me, I am part of the whole, of the pack, of the clan of voices and the thunder of paws, of howls, of death and the joy of the Moon." Lifting the pendant from his neck, he held it to his cheek for a moment before pressing it into her palm.

"May the old Gods be with you, Alcyone, sprite of the sea."

"Strife, you can't do this! Strife!"

Turning away from her, he moved quickly and her fingers reached for empty air as he became a flash of flesh in the trees; a shimmer in the raindrops.

"Strife!"

Dropping to her knees, she pressed her face into her hands and sobbed.

Chapter Seventeen

Cages

THE RAIN POUNDED DOWN in a shower of needles, adding to the fierce determination of his headache. The pack needed him, they were in chaos, half of them waking in panic from their daytime sleep, wondering where he had gone, why he had returned their constant ebb and flow of noise with silence. Shutting them out and meeting with Alcyone had been a mistake. They needed his stability, he was their centre of balance; their alpha.

"I'm here," he whispered to them all. "Shhhh, I am here."

As their howls poured into his head, the familiar screwdriver of pain returned too. Stumbling against a tree, he pressed his head into the trunk, focusing on the crush of the bark against his skin. But the twist of agony tightened and tightened, sending him sliding to his knees. Splayed in the mulch and fallen leaves, he screamed for the hurt to take him away and wrap him in its oblivion. Then there would be no more of this, no guilt, no regret and no more love. As he disappeared into the fireball of pain his wolves tried their best to soothe him, offering him their loyalty, the warmth of their fur and their blood.

Take of our blood. Take it. Take it. Take of our blood, it will make you well, it will make you wolf.

Their chant eased the pain, and as his head cleared he used the tree as a lever against his back to push his shaking legs up to standing. His jaw ached from clenching his teeth and he wiped away a smear of blood that had dribbled from his nose. They were right. He had to become a true wolf. He had waited a lifetime for a family, to be someone important, to be relied on and respected and now if he stayed brave he could have that and more.

If Alcyone just kept away. If she hid in her remote refuge she would be safe.

For a while.

Because Nemesis wouldn't stop at Eristonia, would she? She would seek out every corner of Discordia; she would take it all and give it to the wolves.

I love Alcyone. Can I really let her go?

It didn't matter anymore. Nothing mattered.

Trudging towards the edge of the camp, his exhaustion an iron clamp, slowing him and making him trip and stumble. Tonight would be their night, because tonight the castle would be his. And then he would be ready to be one of them, ready to pledge himself to Nemesis and their new family for whatever destiny eternity would bring them. The wolves guarding the gates bowed as he walked through. Taking the path around the central burrows, out on the other side of the camp towards his hammock, he wondered if this would be his last day in the trees.

Once he'd drunk their blood would he take his rest underground too?

He passed by wolves sleeping nose-to-tail in trenches of mud, their muzzles red and tangled with filth. The smell of greasy fur and rotten meat and something else, a stench of mould and damp and of terrible sadness spiralled from them. It stopped him mid-step and he swayed on the spot as his heart swelled with their misery. Was this all he would feel when he became wolf too? Hunger and sadness?

Stop. It is done, she is gone. I have made my decision.

Near the edge of the camp, cages of prisoners lined the path, their wooden cells guarded by half-burrowed wolves. The large pens were filled with injured half-Gods and humans. These were not just prisoners, they were food to sustain the army and get them ready for their next campaign. As he trudged by, he noticed something new about the smaller cages. They had been lined with fur and covered in leaves, protecting whoever was inside from the worst of the elements. Curious, he peered through the doors of one of the cells. A couple, a man and woman, were huddled in the corner, hugged close together in sleep, a jug of water and a plate of half-eaten meat by their side. Moving along the rows, he could see the same thing. Men and women placed together, in better comfort than the large pens, all of them healthy, with no major injuries. Heart thumping, he stared through the bars of the last in the row, at a couple who were holding a baby, a tiny thing, only a few weeks old. They glared back at him, startled by his face at the door. The woman cradled the child closer to her chest and the man stood in front of them, his hands raised.

Cages filled with couples. And a baby. A new baby.

His anxious fingers reached for the comfort of Zephyrus' pendant but he remembered he'd given it up, that it had gone, that *she* had gone; that he had let Alcyone go. His hands fell back to his sides.

Veering away from the hard eyes of the prisoners, he retraced his steps through the mounds of dirt. He headed towards Nemesis' sleeping quarters where he found her sharpening her spiked spear with a stone. The noise vibrated against the back of his teeth and he had to swallow down a rising coil of bile. She stopped when she saw him, resting her spear onto the ground and leaning into it, her eyes narrowing for a moment before she beamed a wide smile.

"My prince, where did you go? The pack is worried; I have been worried."

"I am here now," he said with a dismissive wave. "I want to know about the new cages, what are they for?"

She passed her javelin from hand to hand before resting it against the wall and turning towards him.

"They are a... necessity for the future. Once these battles are done, we still need to feed our family. These prisoners, they will make this sustainable in the long term. They will be treated well, and they will produce new food sources."

"*Babies?*" he said, stepping backwards.

"We cannot survive on livestock; our pack must have human blood. We will need these… farms. Lots of them. It is unfortunate, I know. But we will look after them while they live and make their end quick, the pups will not be fed to the wolves alive."

"You've hidden this plan from me, hidden this from your thoughts."

"I was waiting to tell you when the time was right, and… well, we all have our secrets, don't we?" She smiled at him, the tips of her incisors peeking out from between her lips, shiny and sharp. "Once you have taken of our blood, once you are wolf, you will understand better. You must stop clinging on to the past, these people are no longer your problem. But you know that now, don't you?"

Sickness washed through him in a wave, making him lightheaded, making him stagger.

A wolf.

He would soon be a wolf. He'd made his decision. He'd let Alcyone go.

Had he? Had he let her go?

"Strife?" she stepped forward, her hand twitching towards her spear and her eyes dark.

"Yes, I have let the past go," he said, keeping his voice steady, though he could feel his body trembling. "I can see everything now, as clear as the night sky."

"That is good. It will bring you much relief to let your old life go."

"It will; you are wise, Nemesis."

"I try my best for you. I always have."

She wrapped him up in a hug and he rested his cheek against hers, holding her tightly. He loved her then, for all she'd done to protect him from Eris, for getting him out of the Pitch and for her bravery; for her conviction. He sent that love through his thoughts and he knew she would feel the force of it before he let her go.

"Could I... could I have a cup of water?" he asked.

"Yes, of course. Come inside with me."

A jug sat on the table in her quarters. The crude wooden cups next to it had been carved by the wolves, the mark of their claws spiralling inside each of them like the whorls of seashells. Emptying his cup quickly, he gulped down another and another until his stomach lurched with too much liquid.

"Do you feel better?" she asked.

"I do. Much better. I'll refill the jug for you before I go." As he stood up, she caught his hand in hers and pulled him towards her.

"Have you really left it all behind you now?" she said, her nails digging into his skin. "Have you let go?"

"I have. I have. I promise," he said.

"That is good news; great news. Once you drink, the headaches will go, and the blood will make you stronger, like one of the first Gods of old! You will live longer, your senses will be magnified... but it also means that you too must feed, do you understand?"

The babies, the babies…

"I do."

"By Erebus, we are almost there! We are on the cusp of real victory!" Her face lit up with a grin and he smiled back, enjoying the sparkle in her eyes. She did care for him, in her own way. That much he knew.

Noon; the wolves were in their deepest slumber and the camp was silent as he took the jug to the pump, filling it to the brim. The bubble of water reminded him of Alcyone's eyes, of their oceanic whirl, of their turquoise, their green and their azure blue. He'd never see them again; never see *her* again. He said his goodbye to her then, his *proper* goodbye. With his eyes closed and his tears dripping into the jug, he whispered that he loved her and would always love her. He wished that the water could send this message to her through her connection to Poseidon, that it could tell her how sorry he was for his mistakes and his flaws. As his tears dried and the water settled, he could see his reflection staring up at him, his eyes were red-rimmed, his hair a mess of knots, and dirt smeared both his cheeks.

He'd just wanted to be part of a family, he'd just wanted to belong.

Nemesis, the wolves, Eris, Alcyone…

Where did he belong?

To all and to none.

Taking a deep breath, he filled his mind with fighting, with battle memories, and with his sword, with his beautiful diamond sword, turning and slicing in the moonlight. The howl of the pack echoed through him and the wolves could hear the same song of victory in their dreams, their connection to him rooted and strong as an old tree.

As he unravelled the vial of rabies from the rag tied to the top of his leg, he blurred out his actions with these thoughts. He shared the ache of his combat-weary body with the pack, with *his* pack. Pulling open the stopper on the tiny bottle, he let a drop splash into the fresh water inside Nemesis' jug, hesitating just for a moment before adding another. Keeping his mind brimming with the battlefields, with the fight, with the smell of fresh meat, he soothed the sleeping wolves. He carried his poison to the troughs of water they would empty as soon as they were awake, adding three drops to each of them as he passed by.

When he got to her hut, Nemesis was sitting cross-legged on the floor, her eyes closed, her face still, lost in her meditations. She didn't even register him as he returned the jug to her table. He set it down gently, making sure he didn't spill a drop, his hand steady and his headache forgotten. He couldn't risk saying anything to her. He couldn't risk her catching hold of anything in his mind so he turned away quickly, slinking back out of the door.

By the time, he arrived at his hammock the Sun had dipped towards night and he knew he only had a couple of turns of the hand to get some rest. Lying back, his body and mind a giant ache, he blinked up at the canopy of leaves and he felt satisfied; clean and light and so… free that sleep arrived deeper and quicker than it had in many Moons.

)(

"I have to go in," Alcyone said. "I have to go into that camp and get him out!"

Their frowns were deep, foreheads wrinkled, mouths downturned and grim. They didn't understand, they didn't *know* him.

"We can't let you do that," Nocturne said, shaking his head. "It's too dangerous."

"We need to make a new plan," Helios said. "We cannot fight Eris *and* the wolves, so maybe we should do as Strife said? Stay and build our own community, a republic right here, away from all of them and begin new dynasties of our own."

"If Nemesis wins she will not stop at Eristonia," Alcyone said. "She wants the wolves to rule here alone, she does not want us to have our own district; we are food, livestock, nothing more. We could be safe here for months, years even, but the wolves will come for us eventually. Pandia, you know this; you have watched them night after night, they are relentless."

Pandia nodded, closing her eyes. "Alcyone is right, I have no doubt they will find us and destroy us."

"And Eris?" Helios asked. "What if the victory is hers?"

"Her iron fist will be absolute, she will have every inch of the city under lockdown. It will be worse than the end of the revolutionary wars when every turn of the hand was filled with public executions and the Pitch was fatter than the city. We will never be able to use the portals again, and if she finds us she will execute us," Nocturne said.

"Then there is no need for further debate," Alcyone said, banging her fist on the table. "I'm going into that camp and I'm getting Strife out. If he still has the rabies virus, I will use it on the wolves myself."

For half a cycle of the Moon, she had done as she had been told—training new troops, surveying the sick, drifting around the camp keeping everyone happy, nodding and smiling like an imbecile. The time had come to do more to protect their future. She was going into the city, and if that meant risking her own life to get there, then so be it. She'd done it before for Zephyrus and now she would do it for Strife.

"They will smell you out like a flower in a field of rats; it is suicide," Pandia said.

"And what is your answer, good Pandia?" she asked. "To sit here and wait for chance to decide which type of Erebus-inspired netherworld Discordia will have in its future?"

"I… I do not have the answer, Alcyone."

"Well, I do! I'm getting Strife out so we can continue with our plan, the one we all agreed to, and you will not persuade me otherwise!"

She watched as they glanced at one another, Nocturne's grip on his sword making his knuckles glow white, Pandia's flint eyes, sad and unblinking, and Helios, her ray of sunshine with a frown sitting on him like a sickness. They were scared but war *was* scary and these were her closest confidants. If they knew her at all they should also know that they would not be able to change her mind.

"If you are intent on making this pilgrimage, I will come with you," Helios said, stepping forward.

"And I," Nocturne said, raising his sword. "You are right. We must do this. We must get him out."

Taking their hands in hers, she smiled.

"Thank you, *thank you,* trusted friends."

"Pandia," Alcyone said. "If we don't return you will take my place here as leader."

"I cannot let this happen," Pandia said. "You must not take this risk!"

"We are at war. You of all people should know that every move we make is a risk," she said. "I need you to share with me all you can remember from your many nights in the city. You must tell us about the camp. I need to know where they sleep, where they eat, where they make water, where they scratch their muzzles. I need to know everything."

"You will not change your mind?" Pandia asked. "You will not think more on this?"

"There is no more time for thinking."

"Okay then," Pandia said. "I cannot fight all of you." Taking a charred stick from the burnt-out fire, she scratched it across the table, drawing a giant circle, with a copse of trees on one side and a single building in the middle.

"As you know, their camp is inside one of the old

training grounds. It used to be filled with grass and flowers but the wolves have ruined it, turning it into a field of mud. They sleep nose-to-tail in a spiral, buried in the earth. There is only one building in the centre of their circle where Nemesis takes her rest, though she's not much of a sleeper. Strife stays away from them, on the edge of the camp, sleeping in a hammock hidden in the canopy of leaves. They have guards posted around the perimeter and the city-facing side has a spiked fence and gate."

"There is only one structure? One building in that whole space?" Alcyone asked.

"The armoury sits just outside their camp but they are not using it. The wolves seem to be happiest below ground. Just beyond the copse of trees are the outskirts of the marshlands, so there will be veins of blood streaking through the soil, which will bring their slumber some… comfort, if that's the right word."

"They sleep all day but are always listening, so if one of them is harmed will they know and will they come to protect their brother or sister?" Nocturne asked.

"Yes," Pandia said, nodding. "The pack's connection and their sense of smell are their greatest strengths. That and their ability to adapt their fighting style to suit their enemy. They are perfect soldiers."

"Maybe our smell is something we can fix," Alcyone said.

"And how will we do that?" Helios asked. "By not bathing for a month? I'm not sure we have that much time."

"By becoming one of them," Nocturne said.

"Exactly!" Alcyone said. "We need to find ourselves three dead wolves, we take on their skin, we run the stink of them into our pores and we hide as closely as we can get to the camp. Tomorrow at noon when the pack is in its deepest slumber, we find Strife."

"Tonight, they will battle, they are close to victory," Pandia said. "They may not be returning to the camp, they might take the castle."

"All the better. Nocturne knows it well, we will rescue him from there," Alcyone said.

"What about Strife's own connection to the pack? He is their leader, their alpha, they will know as soon as we reveal ourselves to him, they will all come to protect him," Helios said.

"He is not yet one of them, he needs to take of their blood to be a true wolf," Alcyone said. "So, he can still hide his thoughts."

"But he has made his decision to be with them. What if he has already drunk their blood? If he has, you will never get him back and you will die," Pandia said.

"Even more reason for us to move quickly," Alcyone said.

"And you know what you must do if he won't come?" Pandia said. "If he is already wolf or he refuses to leave?"

"Yes, I know. But whatever happens with Strife, the plans remain the same, we use the rabies and get out," Alcyone said.

"I will finish it, if it comes to that," Nocturne said.

"No, good Nocturne, if he has to die, it will be by my hand. I saved his life once before and if anyone takes that back from him it should be me."

After saying the words out loud she struggled to find the truth in them. Could she kill him if she had to? The eyes of her generals were always on her; they were smart, that's why she had chosen them and she knew their doubts, but so be it. They would go into the city and they would use their courage to live out their fate like so many dynasties before them. Old words filled her head, the chorus of her mother and father, verses they had lived and died by. Filling her heart with her lineage, with Gaea's great history, she gathered her friends around her, gesturing for them to connect hands.

"Together, in this circle, we are strong," she said.

Nocturne's eyebrows lifted in surprise. Nobody had spoken the rallying words of revolution for over a decade.

"I pledge myself to all of you and you to me. We will fight any enemy who stands in our way and together we will unlock a great new world."

"Together," they said, raising their fists and their smiles. "TOGETHER!"

A thin slice of Moon would make this night the darkest yet of their battles. Hundreds of amber eyes blinked and glinted from across the camp. The shadows were their friend and they had victory within their grasp, with Eristonia ready for the taking.

Nemesis ushered Strife to join her on a wooden bench in front of her hut, her eyes were bright and her face flushed. Standing next to her, shoulder to shoulder, his head felt clearer and more focused than it had for many turns of the hand.

Glancing around the camp, his stomach dipped and fluttered. All the drinking troughs were empty.

"Erebus smiles on us and this darkness will give us our night of triumph," Nemesis said.

As she spoke, the wolves' eyes alighted on him and he repeated her words in his head, cementing them as truth. Nemesis glanced down at him, waiting for him to finish.

"This is the night we will take Eris down," she said, swaying a little as she raised her arms. "Tonight we will celebrate, but this is only the first step and we have many ahead of us. Once the castle is ours and the city is secure there will be more battles to come. We will move our army out to take Alecto's mountains and Tisiphone's deserts. We will secure the kingdom for ourselves, for the clan of wolves."

Will we feed? Will we be sated?

The pack had no interest in castles or mountains or kingdoms, they just wanted meat.

Yes, you will feed.

Something shifted in them, an off note, a slanting wind, a bitter smell.

They were feeling it, they were feeling the sickness.

A wolf rested its head against his foot and he looked down, surprised. Black as dusk with a triangle of white fur on the tip of one ear, this wolf was one of the strongest in the pack. Nemesis kept it near to her, often riding it into battle. It had an intelligence of some kind, a watchfulness, a seeing, and as it pressed its muzzle into his skin, the wolf spoke to him and to him alone.

Home.

Turning its face up towards his, he could see the scratches on its giant blood-stained muzzle. Its eyes were vivid in the darkness and he could feel the suffering it had to live with every day to be in this world.

Home.

A swirl of fire and fountains of lava, black spiky mountains and caves of onyx poured from the wolf's memories into his. In their world, in Hades' realm, they felt no hunger; they guarded the flames, they were happy and secure with their purpose. The clarity of the vision gleamed, bright as a precious stone.

Send us home, alpha. We are ready to go home.

It knew. It knew what he had done.

And it was glad.

As Nemesis raised her arms to the sky, his relief lifted with them. They hated it here. The wolves hated it.

"Tonight, our alpha will take of our blood, tonight when this battle is won he will become wolf!"

A red tear rolled down the wolf's scarred face and it turned away from him to howl at the Moon with the rest of its brothers and sisters.

Hunger. We must feed. We must feed.

Every beast had a role in the loop of life and

afterlife. These wolves were no different. They were as out of place here as he was.

Filled with a fountain of strength, he howled too, singing with his pack. He sent his love to all of them, to all the filthy, murdering beasts who relied on him, who called him their alpha. He had borne them and now he would send them home.

Nemesis wobbled beside him, diamond beads of sweat scattered across her forehead.

"Are you well?" he asked.

"I'm fine, a little tired, that is all."

He nodded, smiling at her. "Tonight, our destiny will take a new turn."

"We are invincible," she said. "The time of the wolf is upon us. Let's go to war!"

The wolf's thoughts had faded into the noise of the pack, but its eyes stayed on him as Nemesis jumped on its back. He nodded and the wolf lowered its head a fraction before turning and galloping away. Pulling his sword from the straps across his back, he tested its weight, slicing the air, getting it settled in the right place in his hand. The pack pulled at him, urging him to move with them and he could feel the illness inside them now, feel it catching hold. Calling to one of the larger wolves to come to him, he joined with the thunder of paws towards the city.

They journeyed fast and unhindered through open gates, slowing a little as they passed along the soft streets of the Flowlands, wary of the silence. Nemesis called to him from the front and the wolves stood at ease as he pushed forward to meet her. The lights of Castle Discord flickered at them from the darkness.

"I don't like this quiet," Nemesis said.

"Shall I scout ahead?" he asked.

"No, but let's keep together, and we move slow."

They inched forward, stepping into the castle's outer courtyard. Something crunched under his wolf's claws and he stopped, jumping down to inspect it. The thin Moon cast such poor light he thought at first that the bricks were smashed but when he bent down he saw fat bundles of broken branches scattered across the road. Picking up a thick twig, the wood felt tacky and an acrid smell spilled from it, making his eyes water. His wolf sniffed at another of the bundles and growled. A glimmer in the darkness caught his eye and when he looked up he could see circles of red popping up in the highest floors of the castle.

"Back!" he roared, waving his sword. "MOVE BACK!"

A cascade of fire arrows lit up the night, arching down towards them, leaving streaks of orange behind his eyes. The oil-covered wood whomphed into flames under the paws of hundreds of wolves. Covering his face with his hands, the heat seared at his skin and he stumbled backwards. His wolf grabbed him in its teeth and threw him in a wide arc away from the blaze. Landing heavily on his back, his breath whipped from his lungs, he struggled onto his elbows. He searched for his wolf, but it had gone, its body a blur of black inside the fire.

"Nemesis?"

"*Still here, my prince.*"

A flash of red cut into his arm and he rolled away, meeting the source of his pain with his sword. He sliced through the Red Guard's neck and its head flew off into the night. Another soldier stepped through the flames and then another. The remains of the pack closed around him, keeping their formation, remaining strong, doing as they always did, protecting their alpha and battling on, gritty and determined. If things were different, if their hunger had been different, they could have been great in this world.

A vryloakas swooped and he carved it in half, a wolf chomping into its chest before it reached the ground.

"Up above the castle, look!" Nemesis said. The fire had caught one side of her dreadlocks, melting them into stumps, making the sharp angles of her cheekbones appear skull-like in the darkness. She pointed her spear to the sky and in the glow of the flames he saw the dragon clinging to the roof of the castle. His mother was perched on its back.

"Come down and face us!" he shouted. "Come down and fight!"

He didn't know whether she heard him but she saw him. She nodded at him and smiled before taking off, white hair whipping at the night sky, flying away from the city towards the mountains. The guards and vryloakas were gone too, they melted into nothing like mist, leaving behind a small huddle of humans inside the circle of crackling embers.

"Hold!" he said, his arms raised. "Hold!"

The pack quivered, muzzles pulled back, snarling.

"What are you waiting for? This is our last battle, once we get through these humans, the castle will be ours," Nemesis said.

"We do not need to fight them. Eris is gone and these people are not soldiers," he said.

"If we cannot kill them now, then we keep them for food," Nemesis said. "They have no other use to us, agreed?"

"Agreed," he said.

Keeping his mind clean and clear of her probing, he turned towards the straggle of humans.

"Surrender!" he shouted. "Your queen has deserted you and you cannot beat us. There is no need for honour when your ruler uses you as battle fodder. Put down your arms."

The soldiers were silent, unmoving.

"Eris has gone. You have nothing left to defend," Nemesis said, stepping up next to him.

The wolves growled, they wanted to eat.

"Come on, do not fight us. Lay down your weapons," he said

The first soldier threw down his knife and the next his sword, then the rest followed, a stream of metal clanking to the ground. With bowed heads, they moved aside to let him pass, some of them sobbing into their hands. Standing in front of the castle, he hesitated, his body like driftwood. He wasn't the same boy who had last walked its halls, who had cradled Zephyrus' dying body to his chest and who had made so many failed promises. Pressing his palms against the doors, he wondered if he would feel something, a soar of pride or the warm glow of victory, but his heart answered him with silence. As his hands slid back to his sides, they left behind a smear of blood on the pane.

The wolves were restless and snarling, not just at the humans but at each other, leaving Nemesis to round up their new batch of prisoners. A large crow was perched just out of reach and he recognised the long scar threading down from its right eye to the tip of its beak. His mother's favourite, still alive and still spying on him. Cawing once, it winked before taking flight, following the path of Eris and her dragon. Glancing behind him at the cluster of men and boys, he wondering what fate awaited them. Breakfast for the pack? Or maybe, just maybe, the pack would be dead before they could eat and Alcyone would find them and protect them. He wondered if her scouts were here now and he scanned the skyline, looking for the tiny girl with hair the colour of moonlight, glancing up at every building, at every window.

Then a familiar rip of agony swallowed him up, splitting through sinew and skin. One of the wolves pushed to his side, letting him lean against it. When the pain finally drifted away again he was left grey and sweaty, clinging to its fur and retching bile onto its claws. Nemesis was right. He would die soon. The black wolf's vision, his land of onyx and lava had been beautiful. If he died would he join his pack there too, or would a different eternity be waiting for him? He was too weary to care anymore. It was in the hands of the old Gods now and he would let them decide his fate.

Chapter Eighteen
Rescue

HOOKS HUNG DOWN FROM the ceiling, trailing over long metal tables. They reminded Alcyone of the stalactites that used to decorate her underground home. The butcher's shop was empty. The family who had lived there were now part of Alcyone's refugee community in the White Plains. The shop had been unoccupied for many days but the smell of raw meat lingered. They had followed one of Pandia's tracked routes into the city, sneaking down alleyways and through dripping tunnels. They arrived at this safe house without seeing another soul. Ghoulish in its desolation, Eristonia's silence lingered on her like a perfume. Were its remaining citizens in hiding or were they dead? The lucky ones who had made it to the White Plains said that many of their neighbours had packed up and run into the mountains. She hoped they stayed hidden until they could make the city safe again, and she hoped they didn't venture too close to Alecto and her bats.

"Can he see us?" Helios said, taking a step back from the window. "I'm sure he looked right at me."

Alcyone took the magnifiers from his hand, turning the glass, making Strife's face clear and bright.

"I don't think so," she said.

Her heart quickened at the distant glaze of his violet eyes and the new scars across his cheekbones. He looked wrong somehow, like a peach coated with green mould after being left too long in its bowl. He was leaning against one of the wolves, clutching his head. Then he screamed with a shriek of pain that made her hands shake, muddying her view so that she had to let the magnifiers rest by her side for a moment before bringing them back up to her face. Strife's hand moved to his chest and her heart jammed in her throat. Frowning, he looked down as his fingers fluttered, searching for something that was no longer there. Her own hands mirrored his movement, finding the pendant he couldn't. Tears burned behind her nose and she smiled. She knew that part of the old Strife, of *her* Strife, was still in there, and that meant he could be saved.

"The fires were a distraction so Eris could get away," she said, giving the magnifiers back to Helios.

"Alone in the night with only a dragon, she is no threat to us now," Helios said.

"Don't underestimate her, my friend, she is smart. Alecto and Tisiphone will protect her," Nocturne said.

"Eris, we will deal with later, for now we must

focus on the task ahead," Alcyone said. "Strife won't be going back to the camp tonight. We will have to find him in the castle. Nocturne, where do you think they will go?"

"The Great Hall is dark enough for the wolves to sleep, and the basement too. But Strife and Nemesis might not want to stay with the rest of the pack and the castle is huge." He rubbed his face, frowning. "Eris has been watching everything unfold from the Pinnacle Room, right at the top of the castle. It has glass walls and ceilings with 360-degree views of the city. If I were to place a wager, that's where I'd say Nemesis will go too."

"Some of the wolves are retreating," Helios said. "At least half are going back out to the city gates."

"They have food at the camp," Nocturne said. "They are keeping prisoners in cages like cattle."

"What about these people, the new ones they've captured?" Alcyone asked.

"They will be used to feed the wolves that remain here," Helios said.

"Then we must free them too if we can," Alcyone said.

Counting the shaggy heads of the remaining group of wolves, she frowned. Twenty-seven. Twenty-seven against three of them. Nine against one.

"I know, I've counted too," Helios said, taking hold of her hand.

"We have trained for this," she said. "Twenty-seven wolves are nothing, nine to one is nothing. Without

Strife, it would have been five hundred to one; a thousand."

"The pack is connected like beads on a string, as soon as we attack one they will *all* know about us," Nocturne said.

"What about the wolves at the camp, aren't they part of that string of beads too?" Helios asked.

"They are. Once we face these ones here, as soon as we are seen, then the turn of the hand starts its count down until the rest of them come to protect their pack."

"Strife has gone inside." Helios stood back at the window with his magnifiers. "What now?"

"There is a tunnel," Nocturne said. "It will lead us to the basement. We start there and make our way up through the stairwell, checking every floor. Once we find Strife, you two must take him to the university and I will get the virus from him and spread it among the wolves. I just hope he still has it."

Alcyone opened her mouth to protest but Nocturne raised his hands, shaking his head. "No arguments."

"We have something else to do first," Helios said, nodding towards the battleground. "We need our camouflage. We need to go skin some wolves."

As the poison flooded their systems, confused and in pain, the pack turned to Strife. They were seeing things, flying swords and red arrows shooting from the Sun. Each wolf's hallucination became the pack's hallucination, magnifying their hysteria. They cried and howled in his head and he lulled and soothed as best he could. A new artery of aggression made them snap and bite at each other. Their hunger had been superseded by a raging thirst that could never be quenched as they were terrified of water. His headache was a constant spit of hot blinding pain and it slowed his step as he stumbled into the castle, trailing on Nemesis' heels. As the Sun rose higher, the pack members that had returned to the camp fell into a restless slumber. Their dreams were of boiling volcanos and of black, black stone.

The remaining wolves leaned against the castle doors as Nemesis picked the locks, their tiredness melting off them like mist. The cool rush of air from the opening doors felt good against his damp forehead as they shoved the shiver of prisoners inside.

"Go and rest, take the prisoners downstairs with you," he said.

The wolves herded their prey towards the basement, but they were thinking only of sleep. The large wolf who had spoken to him went with them, a crust of saliva staining its muzzle.

"Victory!" Nemesis said, lifting her arms and grinning. "The first stage is done and the city is ours. We will need to give it a new name, something fitting for our era. I was thinking of Lykos, which is the name for wolf in the language of the first Gods."

"What about Eris?" he said. "She's still alive."

"She is, and she will turn to Alecto and Tisiphone

to help her. But that is for us to think on tomorrow. Today we take a moment to enjoy our success," she said, her eyes gleaming like river-washed stones. "After so many years waiting and waiting for the time to be right, I can't quite believe this city is finally mine."

A draught circled them, making him shiver as she took hold of his shoulders.

"I have loved you like my own son, good nephew, you know that, don't you?"

"You have always protected me, Nemesis. I would not have survived this world without you."

"Hmmm," she said, nodding. "These pictures, they are beautiful; timeless, don't you think?"

Colourful mosaics covered the circular entrance hall. The scenes his mother had chosen were dark and bloody. Hades with his pitchfork and three-headed dog Cerberus. The Harpies pecking out a young man's eyes, the gore bright in the growing sunlight. And Medusa with her hair a coil of snakes, snarling at a screaming soldier, his body already half turned to stone.

He nodded, saying nothing.

"And this one," she said, stomping at the floor, "this one underneath our feet, do you know *this* story?"

His heart stuttered.

Yes, he knew the story.

The mosaic showed a tall fire-haired woman framed by a circle of blue stones, her raised sword dripping blood. A female figure lay dead at her feet, a crown fallen from her head, a line of red trickling from her mouth.

"Medea," he said, the name catching in his throat as Nemesis pulled him closer, the flush of her fever burning from her.

"The great enchantress who helped the mortal Jason to claim his inheritance and his throne," she said, her grip on him just a little too tight. "Without her, he would never have got away with the Golden Fleece; he would never have claimed his victory. Medea even killed her own brother so they could escape. Did you know that? They chopped him into little pieces and threw him to the sea. Without Medea, Jason would have died on his quest. And how did he repay her? He abandoned her; left her for another. Here, under our feet is the moment she takes her revenge by killing this woman Glauce, whom Jason loved. A tragedy of sorts and one of the greatest stories of betrayal of the first Gods." She twisted her hand around his arm, her fingers digging into his skin.

"And you know all about betrayal too, don't you?"

Flinching as she moved her face close to his, he could see the bitterness in her eyes and smell the sickness on her breath. He tried to pull away but she yanked him back again, hard.

"What have you *done*, Strife? What have you done to my wolves?"

The wolf skins were hot and the stench of spoiled meat made Alcyone's stomach twist. Removing them had been tough work and she could feel chunks of dead wolf skin clogging up her fingernails. The ground snagged at her feet and the shaggy hide felt hotter and heavier than it should. The fur scratched against her cheek and she could see Nocturne ahead of her, swatting and itching his back. The wolf skins wanted gone, they wanted to be back in the ground. They wanted to go back to the life they came from, and they were not going to make it easy on their captors while they kept them here.

Plodding through silent streets, they hugged the apartment buildings, circling the castle. The Flowlands looked paler, as though their bright blue bricks had been faded by the Sun. They needed life and love and laughter inside them, and fresh air to feed their roots. Instead they were sucking in the blood of the dead and veins of red were threading up through the blue. She ran her fingers along one of the houses as she passed by.

"We'll fix this," she said in a whisper, the steam from her breath sparkling on the wall for a second before it melted away.

Sweat dripped down her nose and plinked onto her feet as they trudged through the streets towards the back of the castle.

"How much longer, Nocturne?" Helios asked. "I swear these things are still alive."

"Not much further, we don't know where the wolves are sleeping. I know these furs are a burden but we need to keep them on," Nocturne said with a grunt.

"Not if mine strangles me first," Helios said, winking at Alcyone.

She grinned back, loving him so much then that it

made her heart scrunch into her chest.

"Just here, up ahead!" Nocturne said.

Following a thin trail towards a small locked gate, they climbed over the top, the skins crushing them like shrouds of iron.

"Come," Nocturne said, leading them towards a huddle of spiky shrubs. "Keep your furs pulled tight as you walk through, you might actually be glad of them in here."

Needles scratched at her exposed cheeks as she followed behind, keeping her head ducked away from the brambles. Nocturne stopped deep inside the greenery, kicking at the dirt on the floor to expose a wooden door.

"This will take us to the delivery entrance at the back of the castle," he said.

"How do you know about this?" Helios asked.

"Strife's father built it. It was his personal exit route from the castle. A few of us older guards knew about it. Sometimes Eris would use it too, to remove things, bodies and other items that she didn't want paraded out the front door."

"Do you *really* believe Kratos left me the portal map or do you think his dead body came out of this exit too?" Alcyone said.

"I don't know for sure... but sometimes, when Strife trained with me, I was certain I could feel Kratos close by," Nocturne said. "After you told me about the map and the chiming chains I wanted to hope that he was still alive, but maybe it was just a ghost of him, an echo of his old life clinging to the trees." He pulled open the door and a yawn of darkness spilled out of it, licking at their toes.

"I'll go first, you stay in the middle, Alcyone,' Nocturne said. "Helios at the back. The door at the end will be bolted so we'll need to smash off the lock. Once we're in, we'll scour the basement and work our way up the floors, keeping as quiet as we can, we don't want to wake the pack."

"What about Nemesis?" Helios said.

"If we see her, we kill her," Alcyone said. "We get Strife and we run. If we lose each other we will meet under the Gold Tower, but if you think you have been followed you must hide. We cannot risk being discovered. Agreed?"

"Agreed."

Focusing on the solid width of Nocturne's back, the scar from the bite on her arm throbbed as she thought about all the wolves hiding in the castle. The tunnel fell into darkness and they moved slowly. Dust coated the back of her throat with the flavour of rusty nails. Her mind returned to Kratos and his musical fighting chains. Where was he? What did Eris do to him? She usually boasted of her executions, but about her husband's fate, she was silent. Had she really loved him too much to kill him?

A strong smell of kerosene and a whoosh of flame lit up Nocturne's face making his features ghoulish. A torch flickered from the wall, shining a slither of yellow onto a thin, wooden door.

"Are you ready?" Nocturne said.

"Always," Helios said with a grin, gripping his sword.

Alcyone nodded, her knives in her fists.

Nocturne bashed the door with his shoulder but it didn't give. He tried again but the wood held firm. Helios joined him, both running at it and smashing it with their full weight. They broke through together, falling out into a black corridor that had a fetid stench like rotting teeth. Glittering eyes fixed on her for a second and then rolled away. The wolf staggered, its chest rising and falling with uneven breaths as its twitching muzzle lifted into a snarl. When she took a step closer it whined, cowering into the corner. It didn't look like a monster; it looked terrified.

Helios' sword swooped in a glimmering circle. A curl of blood sprayed across her cheek before its head rolled onto her feet. Its amber eyes stared up at her and its tongue lolled like a snake.

Three more pairs of orange eyes blinked at them from the darkness.

The wolves circled Nocturne, snapping at each other as they stalked closer, slow and clumsy. One of them staggered, almost falling, white foam smothered its snout.

Nocturne looked back at her, his eyebrows high.

They were sick.

By Poseidon, the wolves were sick!

Her first knife moved in a perfect arc, hitting the largest wolf between the eyes. The second throw lodged into the leg of a small, scrappy thing that yelped, bashing into the third, who snapped back at it, growling. They both swayed and the small one reared up, clawing at the air, attacking its own shadow.

Nocturne thrust his sword into its chest and it collapsed on top of him. She rushed over to shove it off as Helios finished the third with a two-armed thrust through the top of its head. The earth rumbled under them, moving quickly to claim the bodies. Like it knew they were coming, as though it had been expecting them.

The wolf skin on her back shivered and pulled, wanting to escape too.

"He did it, Alcyone," Nocturne said. "They are already dying. Strife used the rabies!"

"He did it," she repeated, smiling.

"Thank the Gods, that means I can dump this thing. We don't need a disguise, these wolves don't know what is wolf, human, or half-God," Helios said, throwing his fur to the ground.

Discarding their skins, they picked up speed, following the twist of the basement corridor past the entrance to Eris' interrogation cells. Alcyone touched the surface of the door with her fingers, saying a whispered prayer to Zephyrus' memory as she passed. Spiral stairs led up to the empty entrance hall, the mosaics beautiful in the sunlight. Alcyone stepped over a fresh smear of blood. It was splashed on the tiled face of a dead woman which decorated the floor. She headed towards the Great Hall.

The doors were closed but she could hear noises inside.

They moved closer, weapons raised; listening.

Screams. The sounds inside were screams.

Yanking open the heavy doors, they stumbled into blue-tinged darkness. Moonlight trickled in through the half-open shutters and the bricks were glowing like giant fireflies. Bodies moved in the half-light, twirling and leaping. The wolves were attacking everything, the walls, each other, the chandeliers, their own flesh. The prisoners were huddled together in a corner, watching this macabre dance. One of the wolves clawed at its own ear. It scratched and scratched until it ripped the whole thing off and swallowed it with a dry gulp. It dragged a shrieking man out of the throng of prisoners, shaking him like a rag and then slamming him into the wall with a crunch of broken bones.

"Alcyone," Helios whispered urgently in her ear, pulling her out of her trance. "It is the sickness, they have gone mad!"

"Then let's put them out of their misery."

A large black wolf staggered in front of her. It had a small, grey wolf attached to its neck and its jaws were twisting back and forth, back and forth. Her knife landed in the chest of the black wolf and as it fell the grey wolf flew off to one side vomiting up its feast of flesh in a bloody splat on the floor.

Nocturne and Helios moved in next to her, carving a path through the chaos of bodies. A bitter stink of grease filled the room, making her stomach drop. A moment of hesitation and they were all over her in a swarm, clawing and ripping. One of them pinned her to the ground, grinding its jaws towards her face as she slammed from side to side to avoid its bite, sticking a knife into its ribs. She couldn't pull the dagger free and she thumped at its chest. Its weight pressed down on her, squeezing her breath away.

Glaring up at it, she wanted to meet the eyes of her killer, to see into whatever was left of its soul before it took hers. The wolf's eyes were lighter than some of the others, a burnt umber, like a glorious sunset. Its body was inky black except for its ear which was covered with a triangle of white. She thought of Zephyrus, of her mother and her father, of seeing them again in the next world and she let her fear slide away. Pouring her courage into the eyes of her murderer, she defied it to do its worst.

The umber shifted colour like a forest fire and for a moment the wolf's eyes went black. They disappeared into dark holes where she could see the whole of its hurt, its confusion and its loneliness. The comforting voices of the pack were clogged with sickness and it was lost. Then as it saw her, as it really saw her, a new terror filled its eyes. It jumped away, moving so fast it met Nocturne's sword mid-swing. The force of the blade sliced open its chest, cutting its heart in two. It landed on her feet and she shunted away from the growing puddle of blood.

"Are you okay?" Nocturne pulled her up from the floor, examining her.

"I'm fine, I can't believe it didn't kill me."

Because it feared her, just like the wolf in the basement…

Three more of them rounded on Helios and they were strong. They forced him backwards until his shoulders were pressed into the wall. Nocturne raced to help but she couldn't move. Her mind was filled with a burst of thought.

Not just scared, it had been much more than that.

The wolf had been terrified.

And she'd seen something else in the eyes of the wolf too. A plea; a plea to finish things. To set it free.

The room parted as she stood up and marched through the wolves. The whoosh and thwack of her knives carrying through the air. She joined with Helios and Nocturne, their weapons synchronised as the wolves fell. Stepping back through the litter of bodies, she pressed her fingers to their foreheads, sliding their eyes closed. These beasts should never have been part of this world; they had been dragged here against their will through a stolen sacrifice of blood.

She turned to the prisoners, raising her arms.

"We will get you away from here, we have a camp, far from the city. My friend Nocturne will take you there, he will keep you safe."

"I cannot leave you!" Nocturne said. "This was not the plan we agreed."

"Plans can change and there are only two wolves remaining. They must be with Nemesis and Strife. We can handle them."

He shook his head. "Nemesis might be sick but she is smart, you must be careful."

"You are my most trusted advisor, my general, my place of safety, my rock. I need you to get our army ready for when I return, for when we *all* return," she said, hugging him tightly.

"Whatever you command, I follow, Your Grace," he said, pulling away before she could protest that she was not royalty. That she was only a soldier just like him, a fighter, protecting all that was right and good.

"Come then, Alcyone, we must find Strife," Helios said. "The pack might be broken but their thoughts still flow, there are many hundreds at the camp and they will be on their way to us now."

Nocturne gathered up his refugees, checking their injuries, leading them away from the pile of bodies.

"To the Pinnacle Room," she said. "The top of the castle, let's go. See you back in the plains, Nocturne."

"As sure as day," Nocturne said. "Stay safe!"

Helios' feet were swift, moving in a blur of gold. Keeping her thoughts sharp and filled with his brightness, she ignored the shadows of the stairwell that wanted to suck them into a spiral of black. As they raced higher she could hear a growing noise. A cry of pain which made her skin pull tight against her bones, because she knew that cry, she knew that voice as well as her own.

Strife; they were Strife's screams.

Chapter Nineteen
The Pinnacle Room

NEMESIS SLAMMED STRIFE AGAINST the wall of windows, her forearm pressing into his neck. The glass yielded to him and it felt cold, like a kiss from a pair of dead lips. Growling, one of the remaining wolves staggered forward to protect him. It tripped over its own paws, falling onto its front legs. Frothy saliva dripped from its mouth and its eyes rolled back into white globes.

"What is it? What is this sickness?" she said.

Despite her fever, she had managed to drag him all the way up to the top of the castle. They were in the Pinnacle Room; Eris' giant glass eye in the sky.

"Rabies," he said, choking and pulling at her arm. "Eris' recipe. Fast acting. You don't have long."

"*Rabies?*" She released her grip, brushing at her skin and lurching away as though he were the one infected.

"Why have you done this? You are their alpha. These wolves *love* you."

"The babies; the human babies bred as food. I couldn't be part of that."

"Human babies? Is that what this is all about? What do you care about such things? I thought you had pledged yourself to me, to us, to the wolves!"

"The wolves do not belong here. This is not their world, they want to go back to their realm of onyx and fire. They spoke to me, they want to go home."

"Home?" she said, with a bark of laughter. "Their home is with us, with their brothers and sisters. Home isn't a place, it isn't this castle or a pile of stinking black rocks. Home is family, the alpha and the pack; your pack!"

Who were his pack? Nemesis and the wolves, their voices like a song, loving him no matter what? Or Eris, his first bloodline and his mother? And what about Alcyone? What about the trust in her eyes? The desire for something better sparkling out of them like morning sunlight on water? Which of them were his pack, which of them were his home?

A zip of hurt zigzagged across his face and he rested his hands on the wall to steady himself, but it eased away quicker than before. His pain was disappearing with the last of his wolves.

"I should have pushed harder for you to drink our blood. Then you would have been mine and none of this would have happened," Nemesis said.

She wiped a line of drool from her mouth.

"Anyway, it doesn't matter now."

Reaching inside her tunic, she pulled something

free, a tiny glitter of brightness that danced in her palm.

"Because we can make new wolves."

"No! NO!"

Grabbing for the whistle, he clipped the side of her hand and it spiralled into the air. Throwing his weight after it, he landed hard, the floor peeling the skin from his elbows and knees. It bounced off the tiles and his fingers found it. He wrapped them around the glisten of rubies which pulsated inside his palm like ready to burst boils.

The full force of her boot crunched into his spine and he screamed, the whistle circling away from him. A kick, hard and considered, met his ribs once and then again. He pulled his arms and legs inwards. He protected the soft parts in his middle just like he had as a child when his mother played her games of pain. Scooping up the whistle, Nemesis stood over him. The losses in the pack were coming faster now, one after the other, the wolves' souls spiralling into silence. And his mind felt huge, like an enormous echo. The old emptiness swirled back, filling him with the loneliness he'd lived with for so long before the voices of the wolves came to save him.

"Why aren't you sick?" she hissed, hovering closer, her face beaded with sweat, her melted dreadlocks reeking of burned out fires. "Why aren't you dying too?"

"My mother, she had an antidote, I am immune."

"Then your blood is still clean. That means a new army of wolves can be created, free of this disease. They will be fresh and strong and brimming with power and this time it will drink its fill; this time you won't come back."

"Don't do this Nemesis! If I am dead, who will be their alpha? How will they be controlled?"

"It doesn't matter. Let them do as they please, let them come and destroy. This time Hell will truly spill its heart into the world and it will reign supreme, ending everything that came before. It will find your mother, it will find her generals, it will find all the humans and the half-Gods and they will be nothing more than flesh to fill the bellies of hungry beasts." Her beautiful almond eyes gleamed with a horrible brightness. It swallowed up the part of the old Nemesis that he loved, the Nemesis who had looked out for him, who protected and schooled him, his family and his pack-sister.

"Remember all we have done together?" he said. "Remember the terror of the pack before I joined you? Without their alpha, it will be pandemonium and they will be in pain. This is not the way, Nemesis. Don't let this terrible destruction be your legacy!"

"This is your legacy, not mine. Remember that it is you who poisoned me. It is you who killed your kin. It is you who have committed genocide."

"Yet it is you who dragged them here, where their hunger never leaves them, where they yearn for their old lives, where they don't belong!"

"Which of us does belong, Strife?" she said, swaying above him. "On this Earth created in your mother's image? Neither of *us* has ever belonged here."

He saw then just how similar they were. He saw how she too had been belittled by Eris, kept by her side as a bodyguard while Alecto and Tisiphone were given their own lands to rule.

"Please, Nemesis, please let it go. Let your spirit travel in peace with the wolves to their realm, where you will be with the pack for eternity, where you don't need to fight, where you will be happy. Let me fix this world, let me bring back balance, let me make sure the next generation does belong."

Inside her mind, the pack's demise would be bringing her the same desolation. She would be feeling the same pain, the same chasm of nothing, because Nemesis was like his mirror; his dark reflection.

"You have already helped me on this path. It is our battles and this victory that have cleared the way, let me go, let me set things right," he said. As he spoke, he could see a flicker, a flicker of something behind her eyes. "Please, Nemesis. I know you. I know your hurt like I know my own. Let it go."

"We could have defeated her together," she said, her head in her hands. "Why did you have to ruin it?"

"For peace; for harmony."

"Peace? Harmony? We are of Erebus, we are from darkness. Those are Gaea's words."

"I think they can be our words too," he said.

She rubbed her eyes, shaking her head and swaying.

"You can't leave your pathetic hope behind, can you? It follows you like an unwanted pet, dragging you back, making you weak. If I am dying then why would I bother to save this cursed planet? Why care about a place where good never prevails? Where greed and narcissism grow like weeds no matter how often you cut them down. If you really want peace then you should help me to finish what Chaos' ego couldn't leave to die all those centuries ago."

"I won't do that, Nemesis. If being part of the pack taught me anything it's that a community decides, not one person. We are not pure Gods after all. That's one thing Chaos did do right."

Snarling, she made a grab for him and he sprinted to the door. His outstretched hand brushed the handle as her arm cut across his chest. The air sailed from his lungs, and he could feel the whistle's greed sweeping around him. It whispered to him, soothing him. Just like Nemesis, it told him to be still and to let it feed so the Earth could be cleansed with blood and fire. With a stab of pain and a crunch, it latched onto his neck and he screamed as it burrowed deep into his skin. Staggering away from Nemesis he slid to the floor, watching the whistle melt into its true self. The creature hunched over him. The top of its bald scaly head burned with red sores, its smile revealing rows of pointed teeth. Its eyes were empty black spaces and they held no stories and no history. He could see that this would be the future it gave to the Earth. A blank terrible nothing. Fear yanked at his guts and his heart and his dented soul, wrenching out another scream…

"LET HIM GO!"

Startled, the thing scuttled away, retracting its teeth, staring at a dagger glistening from its shoulder. Another knife landed in its cheek and then its chest. It frowned, dissolving back into the tiny whistle and landing with a plink on the floor, two of its rubies dead and black. As blood spilled from his neck, it glinted at him, still pleading with him to protect it and to set it free.

Another throwing knife landed with a thump in the top of Nemesis' thigh.

A figure stood in the doorway.

Shaking the digging need of the whistle out of his head, he tried to focus on the girl with the knives, because he knew her. Those green eyes, the shade of Poseidon's ocean, and that hair, the colour of sunsets and strawberries.

Alcyone. She'd come for him, she'd come…

Howling, her weapon high, Nemesis charged and he tried to speak, tried to call for her but he couldn't find his voice. Lurching for Nemesis, he stumbled; too slow, far too slow. As she pulled back her spear, he fell to his knees, his words choking from him.

"No! No!"

But Nemesis flinched and scuffled backwards, screaming and cursing. Alcyone's body shone with a dazzling light so bright that Nemesis dropped her weapon to protect her eyes with her hands. The blaze around Alcyone shimmered, transforming into droplets of water. They whirled together into a tornado, growing bigger and faster; whipping at Nemesis, covering her in a lashing spray.

"The water; it burns!" Nemesis said, clawing at her face and throat. "Get her away from me! Get her AWAY!"

Immobile, he watched the power of the ocean tipping from Alcyone, swirling and rushing, changing her into something beyond this world; into a Goddess. And as Nemesis screamed, he remembered his mother's disjointed scrawl on the tiny bottle of poison that had been strapped to his skin for so many moonrises.

Rabies: hallucinations; dehydration; hydrophobia.

Hydrophobia.

A boy appeared from behind Alcyone. He kicked Nemesis' spear out of her reach and pushed her into the wall. The water evaporated into steam and the whistle fell from Nemesis' hand. It slid towards him, landing against the toe of his boot. It called to him with its song of fragmented love, filling him with its need, ready to wipe away all his pain like a polishing cloth.

"Strife? Can you hear me?" Alcyone called to him, concern creasing her forehead into a perfect 'V' like a wishbone.

Leaning forward, his fingers brushed against the top of the whistle. He could hear the final dying howls of his pack, who were still running to help him but would never reach the castle. Collecting the whistle inside his hand, it burned hot with promises. The whistle would take all his worries and destroy them in its fires. It would be the only friend he could ever need, the *best* friend he could ever have. If he let it drink his blood, just a little, it would save him, it would keep him alive. It could be his sanctuary and his home. The face of the demon, teeth chattering, flickered in and out of focus, the call of the whistle scratching at the many scars on his heart. It promised him it could heal them, that it would cast them into Lethe's waters of forgetting. And underneath all this, like the hum of a bee, he could hear Alcyone's voice. She called and called his name as the glass walls of the Pinnacle Room expanded and contracted around him like giant lungs.

The whistle shifted its shape again. It twisted into a beautiful woman with black hair like tar and purple eyes like his; into Hera; into victory. The goddess smiled, holding out her hand to him, golden bangles circling her arms. A new army was expecting him, waiting to fill the lonely void in his head with their howls and their obedience and their love. Hera knew the music of oblivion and if he'd only listen, she could teach him the tune. Nodding, he smiled and touched her outstretched hand. He really wanted to learn these songs, more than anything he'd ever wanted before.

"STRIFE!" Alcyone said. She reached for him, and he grabbed her wrist, twisting her knife out of her fingers. "You're still in there, Strife. I know you are. That's why I'm here, that's why I came to find you. Come back to me."

The boy with the golden hair took a step closer, his sword in his hand.

"Stop Helios! Wait!" Alcyone said and the boy hesitated.

Pressing the point of the dagger against her neck,

he could feel her pulse, fast and strong underneath his fingers.

"This isn't you, Strife. Come back. Come back."

Nemesis howled, her voice the only one left now of the pack, of his family of wolves, his community, gone now; all gone.

So, tired, so, so tired.

Tears were filling Alcyone's eyes, changing their colour again; green and blue; green and blue. A prickle of blood bloomed under the sharp tip of the dagger and Hera's radiant smile widened.

That's it, do it, kill her. She is nothing; needless; flotsam and jetsam.

"Come back to me Strife," Alcyone whispered. "Come home."

Home.

Home.

He raised his boot and she cowered away from him, arms over her head as his foot blasted down. Each slam cleansed him, leaving him light and free as he smashed and smashed and smashed the whistle into tiny splinters of red and gold. The ghost of Hera shrieked with the wrath of Erebus himself but he didn't listen. He didn't stop until Alcyone grabbed him and told him that it was done, that it was over. Sobbing, he let her hold him, let her circle him in her arms as he choked up all his grief for Zephyrus, for Nemesis, for the wolves; for all of it.

"I'm sorry, Alcyone. I'm sorry you had to come for me," he said.

"I don't want you to be sorry, I just want you to

stay out of the darkness. Can you do that? Can you keep to the light?"

"Yes, if you stay with me, then I can. I am yours, Alcyone," he said, placing his hands over hers. "*You* are my home. Always."

"Always," she said, smiling.

Lifting his head in her hands, she smoothed away his tears before placing Zephyrus' pendant back over his head. It came to rest, a perfect fit, in the hollow of his neck.

"Shall I finish her?" Helios said. "It would be doing her a kindness." His sword glinted as it pressed it against Nemesis' heart and she whimpered, her body shaking with fever.

"No, please! Wait!" he said. "She is the last of my pack, I need to do this for her. It is my place to give her rest, not that of a stranger."

Helios looked at Alcyone.

"Good Helios," she said. "Nemesis is Strife's family, he should be the one to send her on her last journey. Let us respect this honour."

Helios stepped back, bowing his head as Strife knelt next to Nemesis. Smoothing the remains of her ruined hair from her forehead, he shushed her like a baby. He wiped away a crust of white from her mouth with the corner of his sleeve.

"That girl, she has powers I have not seen in a half-God, she has something given to her from the first-Gods. Who is she?" Nemesis said.

"She is Alcyone, daughter of Asclepius and Amphitrite."

"The dead boy's sister? Then she is of Gaea's line."

"She is," he said with a half-smile.

"You plan to bring our dynasties together?" she said, her eyes bright and lucid. "We are separate for a reason, it isn't how things are done, it isn't the old way."

"The old way? By the Gods, Nemesis, look how doing things the old way turned out for us."

"You have too much good in you, Strife. Too much… conscience."

"I'm not going to let shadows that feed on doubt guide my path anymore, Nemesis. You did your best for me. For that, I will always be grateful."

"Without me, without the wolves, you have no army. You have nothing."

"I have plenty," he said.

"Remember Phoebe?" she said, taking hold of his arm, her grip too tight. "That poor broken girl, imprisoned for nothing, tortured for nothing? That is how this all ends. Your mother will brutalise and kill *all* your friends and she will make you watch before she kills you too. Do you think a few child soldiers can save you?"

"I don't know, Nemesis. I don't know how this will end, but the path I will take is the *right* one and that is all that matters."

"Then you are a fool."

"Maybe so, but that is my choice. Now, I will do you the same kindness that you gave to Phoebe back in that cell not so many moonrises ago. It is time to quicken this. Do you want to say the last words, or will I?"

"You say them, my prince," she said with a sigh, the ghost of her old self passing through her smile. "I am ready to join our wolves, I am ready for the long journey."

"Go well, Nemesis, go well into the next world; go well and prosper."

The blood gushed fast and thick and she shuddered, legs kicking. He cradled her head in his lap, keeping a tight hold of her until it was done.

"Goodbye, Aunt Nemesis, my pack-sister." A new scar nicked his heart as he closed her eyes.

"We need to go," Alcyone said, resting her hand on his shoulder. "We are not safe here alone. We must get back to the White Plains."

As he stood up, the light in the Pinnacle Room dimmed and lifted. Alcyone's face disappeared into shadow and then came back to him. Blinking, he looked up at the ceiling as a slither of black slid across the room. The wind blustered, shaking the glass, stretching it in and out.

"Is it a storm?" Alcyone said, gripping his hand. "Where are the clouds?"

"I… I don't know."

Darkness scudded across the sky and it was not of thunder, but of wings. Enormous black wings. Claws clattered onto the stretched glass, puncturing it. Long talons followed behind, curving down, catching Helios by the back of the neck and dragging him screaming into the air. Alcyone shrieked, reaching for him, but he'd already disappeared. Alecto's bats, hundreds of them, were cascading across the sky like giant locusts. More landed with a thump, scratching and squealing, peeling open the Pinnacle Room's roof like the skin from an orange. Alcyone stood frozen, her hands grasping for empty air. Grabbing her by the waist, he pulled her close to him.

"Helios! We have to get him back!"

"We must go before they take us too," he said as she stared at him, her mouth slack. "Alcyone! Can you hear me? We have to go!"

Gloom slicked into every corner and more and more bats gazed down on them, their eyes a constellation of rotting stars.

"We have to run, Alcyone. We have to run!"

"Strife?" her grip on his hand crunched into bones and time's breath stopped. A lock of her hair lifted, twisting up inside a huge misshapen talon.

"No! NO!"

Before he could grab his sword, a tattooed arm yanked Alcyone into its embrace, leaving the bat hissing at its lost prize. The man weaved her away from the reaching claws, slashing at bats with a curved, copper sword topped with a beautiful sapphire hilt.

"Strife, you must both come with me now!" The man spoke his name with a voice he recognised. A deep voice that weaved its way up through long-buried memories.

"Father?" Strife said, shaking his head, not believing it, not knowing if the shadows were playing their old tricks. "*Father?*"

"My son. *My son.* I am so proud of you." Kratos smiled at him. "Eris locked me out of the city, she cursed my soul and placed the spell inside that shrine in the armoury, the shrine of my sword. And you smashed it, you set it free; you set me free."

Strife stared at this man he never thought he'd see. This man that his mother had kept from him. Kratos moved Alcyone behind him and reached out for Strife. He took hold of his father's strong hand, took it and squeezed it tightly.

The bats smeared themselves over the glass, and as he watched them squatting above him dread filled him like boiling oil.

They were blocking out the light, blinding their prey, swallowing the room into darkness.

And, once they did, the three of them were as good as dead.

THE END OF BOOK ONE

Author's Note

The wonderful stories that humans weave to both make sense of our world and to escape it have sparked my imagination since I first creaked open the spine of an Ursula K Le Guin book many years ago.

Greek mythology in particular left me wanting more. What else happens in the lives of all these amazing characters? As a quiet and shy child, the gods and their offspring were such a huge part of my inner life that I itched to *really* know them. Their stories, their personalities, their emotions… the classics, to me, were just skirting on the surface of a much deeper world.

So, I decided to forge my own journey for some of them in *The Army of Wolves.*

There are more adventures to come for Strife and Alcyone, and I hope you continue to follow them with me. If you want to be the first to know when the next book, *A Fury of Bats* is released and read a little more about their universe, join my readers' club and download the free story of the archer, *Atlanta* here:

www.clairemoore.co.uk/atlanta

If you liked this book, I would be so grateful if you could leave me a review on Amazon. Authors really need reviews - almost as much as Strife's wolves need blood!

Go well and prosper.

Claire Moore

Coming Soon

Book two in *The Half-God War* series: *A Fury of Bats*

Readers' Club Download Offer

Join my Readers' Club and get a free copy of my short
story, "Atlanta"

www.clairemoore.co.uk/atlanta

Find out more about me:
www.clairemoore.co.uk